The Merriman Chronicles

Book Five

The Threat in the Baltic

Copyright Information

The Merriman Chronicles - Book 5

The Threat in the Baltic

Copyright © 2015 by Roger Burnage

With the exception of certain well known historical figures, the characters in this book have no relation or resemblance to any person living or dead.

All rights reserved. This book and all "The Merriman Chronicles" are works of fiction. No part of this book may be reproduced or used in any manner without written permission of the copyright owner except for the use of quotations in a book review.

Sixth Edition – 2024

Updated by: Robin Burnage
Edited by: Katharine D'Souza

ISBN: 9798344322346 (Paperback)
ISBN: 9798344322711 (Hardcover)

www.merriman-chronicles.com

Books in the series

James Abel Merriman (1768 – 1843)

A Certain Threat

The Threat in the West Indies

Merriman and the French Invasion

The Threat in the East

The Threat in the Baltic

The Threat in the Americas

The Threat in the Adriatic

The Threat in the Atlantic

Edward James Merriman (1853 - 1928)

The Fateful Voyage

Chapter One

Capture of French Corvette

Spring, the year 1800

"Deck there, something on the starboard bow. A frigate I think, sir, no masts anyway."

The lookout's hail was clearly heard in the great cabin of His Majesty's frigate Lord Stevenage. Her captain, James Merriman, was trying to complete his report for the Admiralty on the events in Bombay and the Indian Ocean. His memory seemed to be playing tricks and he had just paused in his work, realising he had omitted to include full details of the capture of the first frigate in one of the enemy Indian ruler Tipu Sahib's shipyards.

Glad of any respite from his tiresome task, he hurried up on deck to find his officers gathered in a group on the quarterdeck. The third lieutenant, Shrigley, was racing up the ratlines like a monkey to the mainmast head. Taking a place by the lookout, who shuffled sideways to give him room, Shrigley opened his telescope and quickly found what the lookout had seen.

"Captain, sir," he shouted, "definitely a small frigate but with its topmasts and mainmast gone. She is flying the French colours, sir."

Merriman nodded. "Thank you, Mr Shrigley, stay there and keep me informed of what she will do. Mr Andrews, beat to quarters if you will, I'll take no chances."

"Aye-aye, sir," replied the first lieutenant, shouting the order.

A young marine drummer immediately began the drumroll bringing about what to a landsman would seem to be a bedlam with men running in all directions at once. Crashes and bangs from below signified that all partitions, furniture and chests were being sent down below to clear space all along the gundeck from stem to stern. Men were gathering in their stations at the guns and others waited beneath each mast, ready to go aloft to furl sail or whatever the Captain ordered.

The marines assembled on the quarterdeck and fighting tops with their officers. On the order they began to load their muskets. The bedlam resolved itself in minutes.

"Mr Andrews, have the starboard battery loaded with round shot and run out ready. We'll approach her cautiously from astern."

As the *Lord Stevenage* neared the French ship, she fired a single cannon shot but kept all her gun ports closed. A white flag replaced the Tricolour on the stump of the mizzenmast.

"By God, sir, the Frenchies are surrendering without a fight," exclaimed the marine captain, Edward St James. That one shot came nowhere near us."

"Probably fired for honour's sake so that they couldn't be accused of surrendering without a shot being fired," replied Merriman. "But remember the old saying, 'Bees that have honey in their mouths have a sting in their tails.'"

The French ship could be seen to be rolling heavily, broadside on to the waves and with no sails to give stability. Beyond, the French coast was a grey line on the horizon and, without help, the ship was sure to strike the rocks. As *Lord Stevenage* moved closer still the ship's rudder could be seen swinging from side to side with the ship obviously not under control. The name was clearly painted on the stern, *La Aigle Francaise*.

"Not looking to be much of an eagle now, sir," remarked the acting fourth lieutenant, Gideon Small.

"Indeed not, Mr Small. You will go across with me. Mr Andrews, Mr St James, prepare parties for boarding, marines and armed seamen. I will go across with them."

The French captain was visible on the quarterdeck surrounded by his officers so Merriman seized a megaphone and shouted out, using the French he had learned from one of his prisoners in an earlier action some years ago.

"Capitaine, I know you are flying a white flag but if there is any sign of treachery I will fire into you. Do you understand?"

The Frenchman waved his arm and shouted back, "Oui, m'sieur, we will not resist."

Boats were quickly lowered and filled with the boarding parties. On the crossing between the two ships, Merriman ordered a petty officer and some men as well as Captain St James and some of his marines to secure the ship's magazine.

Climbing onto the deck of *La Aigle Francaise* surrounded by his seamen and marines with fixed bayonets, Merriman found the French crew sitting miserably on the deck with no weapons in sight. The captain and officers stood in a group to greet him. The captain stepped forward, introduced himself as Henri Labourd, and offered Merriman his sword.

"Thank you, Captain. My name is Merriman, James Merriman. You, Captain, may keep your sword but your officers should surrender theirs to this officer."

They gloomily complied and St James soon had his arms full of swords which he passed on to his men.

Merriman looked about him. The French ship was not a frigate but rather a corvette, a small frigate. The ship's mainmast had gone, leaving only a stump, and on both foremast and mizzen the topmasts had also gone. Strangely the ships' boats seemed to have survived stacked amidships.

He turned to Captain Labourd. "What happened, sir? Your ship is in a mess."

"Well, sir, we managed to slip out of Brest but a gale sprang up and your blockading ships were forced out to sea. Then a week later the wind changed, my ship was taken aback and the masts went overboard. If I had had a competent crew it would have been avoided," said Labourd bitterly. "Most of them are not even seamen, men rounded up in the port and ordered aboard at bayonet point. They were reluctant to carry out their orders even if they could understand them. Even some of my officers have come from the army with no experience at sea at all. The best men are the junior officers, what you call petty officers, but they were too few. Could we talk alone?" he asked, moving towards the bulwarks.

There they were alone, apart from Merriman's bodyguard of his cox'n, Matthews, and two marines, ready for any sign of treachery. Labourd said, "I wanted to fight you but with my ship in such a condition I thought it would be a waste of lives. We are helpless to drift and couldn't fight as I would have done. Damn that fellow Napoleon Bonaparte, he thinks nothing of the navy. We have been denied spares of every kind. All he thinks about is his army. We have some of your English seamen secured below, I think fifty or so, they can be released. I would have ordered this done sooner but with no English officers I feared they would start to fight us."

By now they were speaking in English in the hope that none of the French would understand, but they were mistaken. Suddenly one of the officers drew a dagger and ran at Labourd screaming, "Labourd, you are no true Frenchman, you are a traitor and you must die." The man was spitted on the marines' bayonets before he got near either of the captains, but he managed to throw his dagger which struck Labourd on the shoulder though it did no damage. The marines picked up the man's body and pitched it overboard.

Merriman had been thinking about what he should do next and he quickly decided. "Captain Labourd, I am going to take your ship in tow with a crew of my own men and some of your prisoners. There are too many of your own men for us to guard safely all day and night so I propose to send them ashore except for fifty who will be confined below. Your boats appear to be in good order so they should have no difficulty but the men may have to be taken in two journeys. Your biggest boats have sails I expect, which will speed it up. Meanwhile you must select some of your real seamen, perhaps your petty officers, to stay behind to help secure the tow. My marines will be alert for any signs of trouble. You and your officers are my prisoners and will be secured aboard my ship."

"Thank you, Captain, I don't think you will have any trouble. My men are thankful that there has been no fighting and will be happy to do as you say, glad that they will not be prisoners."

So it happened, the French crew were ferried ashore and the English prisoners released. They staggered up on deck, blinking in the strong light. All of them looked half-starved and some had to be helped by their comrades.

"Lieutenant Andrews," said Merriman, "have the doctor brought over at once to see to these poor fellows, and have the cook started preparing food for them."

"Aye-aye, sir," responded Andrews, already shouting orders as he turned away.

Merriman turned to the ex-prisoners. "Men, you have nothing to fear now. My ship's surgeon will be here shortly to examine you all and food is being prepared for you. A tot of rum will cheer you up, I shouldn't wonder. Now then, I want you to tell Lieutenant Small who you are, your rating, what ship you were on and how long you have been in captivity. Mr Small, you will attend to this. Doubtless you will find paper and writing materials in the captain's cabin. Sit down, you men, and wait for the doctor to attend to you."

One of the men, tall and fair-haired, stepped hesitantly forward and touched his forelock. "Captain, sir, may I speak?"

"Yes, yes, speak out man, what is it?"

"Sir, my name is Sorensen, sir. I'm Swedish and I was a seaman, rated Able Seaman on board the old *Argonaut* under Captain Edwards and you were a Midshipman then. These men have asked me to speak for them, sir, to thank you for releasing them from the Frogs. We'll do whatever we can to help your prize crew tho' not all of us are strong enough. The Frogs starved us, sir."

"Very well then, Sorenson, thank you for that. What rank or rating are you now?"

"Master's Mate, sir," the man replied.

Just then Doctor McBride climbed aboard with one of his assistants and began to examine the men. As he did so, he muttered words doctors the world over would say, "Hmm, hmm, very good, a'ha, that wound needs some attention, how long is it since your arm was broken, I don't like the look of that," and other such comments. He sorted the men into three groups and then reported to Merriman.

"Most of them are well enough, sir, although most of them are weak and need feeding up. Some of them have wounds that will need immediate attention and three of them have very serious wounds, I fear that one of them will not see tomorrow's dawn. His wound is badly infected and gangrene has set in."

"Thank you, Mr McBride, have a look below to see what this vessel has as a sick berth and treat them here. Feel free to use any of the French materials you find."

Meanwhile, a party of English seamen with a bos'n's mate set about repairing the broken tiller. "Soon have that fixed, sir. The old one was rotten at the inboard end, no wonder it broke. We can fix that with a new piece of timber," reported the bos'n's mate.

Another party, helped by the remaining Frenchmen and some of the released prisoners, secured a thick hawser floated over from Merriman's ship. That took several hours. Meanwhile, the bos'n and some seamen managed to rig up trysails on ropes from the top of the lower foremast and the mizzen lower mast and to re-rig a spanker on the rear of the mizzen mast. All the time Merriman kept a keen watch on the French coast to which they were drifting ever nearer.

At last all was done that could be done, the French officers secured in the gunroom on *Lord Stevenage* and the petty officers and fifty of the best seamen secured below in the French ship under an adequate guard of marines. Then came the difficult bit.

Sail was set on *Lord Stevenage* as well as the pitiful small sails on the prize. Progress was slow. At first it seemed that the ships weren't making any headway but slowly they began to move further out to sea. Merriman had left Lieutenant Henry Merryweather in command of the tow with Lieutenant Shrigley, but all went well. Fortunately the weather never gave more than a stiff wind and Merriman ordered more sail set before staggering below, completely exhausted, and collapsed into his cot unaware that his servant Peters covered him with a blanket.

Merriman appeared on deck again as the dawn light was beginning to show. He had been woken by the noise of the crew going to action stations. That was the normal activity on board Naval vessels at dawn in case the increasing light showed an enemy ship nearby. There were none and so the crew were ordered to stand down to start the endless routine of maintenance and cleaning.

"Good morning, sir. I hope you managed a few hours' sleep," said a grey-faced and exhausted Lieutenant Andrews who had kept the deck together with Midshipman Green.

"Good morning, David. I did, which it seems is more than you two did. How is the tow, any problems in the night?"

"No, sir, none at all. She is following like a lamb after its mother, as you can see."

"Very good, David, now you and Mr Green can go and get your heads down."

Merriman had been aware of his servant Peters hovering nearby carrying a steaming jug of coffee. "Freshly brewed coffee, sir? And your breakfast will be ready soon".

"I'll be down shortly, Peters, for breakfast and a shave". But he took a cup and then he turned to the Ship's Master, the recently promoted Tom Henderson, originally a Master's Mate under the old Master, Mr Cuthbert, who had his legs cut away by a round shot in an action with pirates off Ceylon some months earlier.

"Mr Henderson, did you have a good night? Good, now you will have to take command with Mr Small while I go below for breakfast and a shave. The weather looks good so I don't think you will have any trouble. We should soon see some of our ships on blockade duty so keep the lookouts alert for any sail."

"Aye-aye, sir. You can depend on me, sir," replied Henderson, touching his forelock.

"I know that Mr Henderson or else you would not be here," said Merriman, disappearing below.

Peters had been keeping an eye open and, as soon as Merriman went down, he emerged from the galley with a dish covered with a towel. "Your breakfast, sir, your favourite. Pork fried in biscuit crumbs and there is more coffee, sir."

After breakfast and a wash and shave, Merriman put on clean clothes and went on deck, quite satisfied with life. *Lord Stevenage* was pulling strongly on the *Aigle Francaise* which was following docilely in her wake. The sun was shining, the wavelets sparkling and Merriman wondered how long it would be before he saw home again. His thoughts turned to his wife Helen and his little son, now over two years old. A letter from Helen he'd received in Bombay had told him that both his mother and father had died soon after he sailed for India. His mother had been unwell for months and her death was expected but his father had been expected to live much longer. He shook his head and returned below to carry on with writing his reports.

Chapter Two

To Portsmouth with prize Corvette

Captain Merriman was feeling very proud. Things had happened so quickly after his ship entered the outer harbour at Portsmouth. The crews of other ships had begun cheering at the sight of the French corvette, flying the French flag with the British flag flying above it. The formal gun salute was fired to the Port Admiral's flag and then, as the French ship reached the spot indicated by the harbourmaster's launch, the tow was cast off and the skeleton crew of British sailors dropped her anchor assisted by some of the Frenchmen under marine guard.

The topsails on *Lord Stevenage* were hauled round into the wind and backed to stop her in exactly the right place where she too dropped anchor. The sails disappeared like magic into a tight harbour furl and the ship was at rest for the first time since leaving India many months before.

Merriman knew that many telescopes would be looking from the shore for any sloppy handling of the ship but he also knew that his officers and men were so well trained that no watcher would find anything to criticise.

The anchor had barely touched bottom before Signals Midshipman Green shouted, "Signal from Flag, sir, our number. Captain and passenger to report to Flag at once."

"Thank you, Mr Green, have my boat called away".

There was no need for that last order as Merriman's cox'n Matthews already had the boat's crew ready. They were wearing their best uniforms, bought especially for them by Merriman, so that they and the boat looked as smart as new paint. The boat was quickly in the water and Merriman, clutching an armful of reports and wearing his best uniform, looked round for the passenger who was to go with him.

The passenger was none other than Mr Laurence Grahame. Grahame worked for the Treasury Department, under the direct control of Lord Stevenage, who in turn reported directly to the Prime Minister William Pitt the younger. At that time, the Treasury Department was responsible for England's agents abroad, spies really, on whom the country depended to pass information from Europe's capital cities and ports which could help England in the ongoing struggle with Napoleon Bonaparte.

Mr Grahame was ready and, knowing what was expected of him, climbed down into the boat with Merriman last as tradition demanded, to the usual squealing of the Bos'n's whistles and a cloud of pipeclay as the marines smartly presented arms. Merriman and Grahame had worked together on several adventures in the past, in the Irish Sea, Ireland, the West Indies, and latterly in India. All these events had been successfully completed. Indeed, the two men worked well together, so much so that Grahame, who was one of the Treasury's top agents, asked the Admiralty for Merriman to join him in his forays abroad.

As the boat sped over the water at Matthews urging, Merriman took a moment to look back at his ship to be sure that everything was as it should be. Then he smiled, he knew that the skies would fall before First Lieutenant Andrews would miss anything. The sails were all tightly furled, the yards were exactly square and level and he had seen the various parties of seamen on deck doing all the last minute things needed. Turning back to the land, he looked round him for anything new. High on a hill was a strange structure consisting of three sturdy uprights sticking out of the roof of a small building, with octagonal panels between them. Even as he watched it appeared that the panels moved in some kind of order.

He drew Grahame's attention to the sight, asking, "What do you make of that weird thing on the hill over there?"

Grahame studied it through the small pocket telescope he habitually carried. "It could be one of the new signalling stations. They were being talked about when we were here last, but perhaps we will know soon enough."

On arrival at the Admiralty offices, clearly designated by the Admiral's flag flying above, they were ushered by a lieutenant into a waiting room already occupied by several other officers.

Some of them were obviously senior as they wore the two bright epaulettes indicating that they had been Post Captains for at least three years, compared to the single epaulette Merriman wore on his right shoulder. The lieutenant disappeared but returned a few minutes later with a message. "Captain Merriman, sir, Admiral Fitzherbert's compliments and he regrets that you must wait until he has seen these other Gentlemen first. However I can tell you that you are required to go to the Admiralty in London as soon as possible."

"Very well, Lieutenant," replied Merriman. "We are well used to waiting in the navy. But how do you know that we have to go to London? We have only just arrived."

"Oh, that's easy, sir. With the new telegraph system we can send a signal to the Admiralty in as few as seven or eight minutes and have a reply equally quickly. Sometimes it takes longer due to rain or fog preventing clear sight of a signal tower from the next in line. Orders have been waiting for you ever since your ship was seen in the channel. This new telegraph system is wonderful; you may have noticed the new construction on the high ground? That is part of it."

"Yes, we did. Of course we had heard of it but I don't believe it was fully ready before we left for India more than two years ago."

Eventually Merriman and Grahame were ushered in to the Admiral's office where he was seated at a large, chart-covered desk. He rose to his feet and welcomed them with a smile and a handshake. "Sit down, gentlemen. I'm vastly pleased to see you back again from your adventures in India, Captain. All went well I hope?"

"Indeed it did, sir. I think I may say that it went very well. The East India Governor in Bombay expressed his satisfaction and thanks for our help."

"I know you were sent out there at the request of the Honourable East India Company who had suffered increasing raids on their commerce by pirates on land and sea. As I remember it you were also tasked with finding out what you could about that fellow Tipu Sahib's plans to build the biggest fleet of warships in the East, and to tell the Company about

Napoleon's plans to attack India. Of course Boney's plan for India came to nothing when his army was defeated in Egypt and his fleet destroyed in Aboukir Bay by Admiral Nelson. I believe he crept back to France with his tail between his legs. Now what were you able to do out there?"

"Well, sir, we destroyed many pirate dhows, captured one of the principal pirate leaders, and destroyed several larger vessels including some under construction in Tipu's shipyards. The men and ships of the Bombay Marine were of great help in this and we captured two frigates. The Company wanted to buy them both in for the Marine. As I couldn't bring them back here I agreed. The Governor said that payment would be made from the Company's offices in London. I have a letter from him to the directors in London to that effect. Certainly no money was given to us, sir. As far as French spies and their agents are concerned, Mr Grahame can tell you more."

"Of course, Mr Grahame, that is why you were sent to India, to seek out such people. I apologise, sir, for not bringing you into the conversation before. I've been talking too much myself."

Grahame smiled. "There is little to report, Admiral. I found several villains and investigated some of Tipu's shipyards but, as you will know, Tipu's death in the battle of Seringapatam put a stop to his dream of building a fleet and there was little left for me to do after that," he said modestly.

"I'm sure that was not all, sir, but I won't push you further. And now, Captain, I want to hear all about the capture of the French corvette you brought in, but first…" He bellowed for the Lieutenant who nearly fell over his own feet such was his haste to find out what he was wanted for. "Some wine for my guests, Archer, and be quick about it."

When all were settled with a glass of rather good claret in hand, the Admiral nodded to Merriman to start, but he said, "None of the long-winded stuff you will have put in your report, just give me the main points."

"Well, sir, it was really all too easy. There was no battle or fighting involved. We sighted the ship drifting on to a lee shore with only the lower foremast and lower mizzenmast still standing, her remaining rigging in tatters and her rudder not working. I rounded to astern of her, they fired one shot for honour's sake and then they hauled down their flag and surrendered. I went aboard with some armed men and was met by her captain who formally surrendered his sword. Apparently he had managed to take his ship out of Brest during an offshore gale. Our blockading ships had been blown off station and he thought he had got away cleanly but a few days later the wind changed rapidly and the ship was taken aback and lost her masts. Very few of her crew were real seamen and I think he and his men were pleased to be captured without a battle which they could not have won with their ship in such a bad state. We found English prisoners aboard, all had been badly treated and half starved. Two of them died but the rest of them are much recovered."

"An excellent account so far, Mr Merriman, but tell me, did you find out where the Frenchie was going?"

"All I could find out, sir, was that she was to join with a small French frigate squadron going to the West African coast to attack our convoys. The English prisoners were to be sent to some French possession in South America."

"I see, Captain, what did you do with the French crew?"

"I already had determined, sir, to try and take the ship in tow to save her from going ashore on the rocky shoreline. Her surrender made it easier to have a hawser dragged aboard her and secured, indeed the French worked with a will knowing that if we left them they would be blown onto the rocks and many men drowned. Of course my marines were there in case they wanted to fight but none did and as most of their boats were still intact I put most of the seamen ashore. There were too many of them to guard safely. I kept the officers and most of the warrant officers as well as fifty seamen as prisoners and they are still aboard the ships now. I hope that I can deliver them into your hands, sir, the Captain and his officers gave their parole but not the others. In fact one of the junior lieutenants turned out to be an ardent revolutionary and tried to kill his captain for surrendering but he was killed by my marines before he could do so."

The Admiral had been listening closely to Merriman's account and remarked, "It must have been hard to tow her I think."

"Yes, sir, it was. She rolled like a log and tried to go her own way like a pig, but once my men aboard had managed to repair the rudder and stretch sails from the stumps of the foremast and mizzen mast, it wasn't too difficult. The biggest worry was the fear of more gales or even meeting another French ship of war but the weather was kind and I didn't really expect to meet a French warship, sir. I have my written report here, sir. I have a copy of it together with my detailed report of our actions in the Indian Ocean for the Admiralty."

"Very well done, Captain. I think it is safe to say that if your prize is in good order apart from the masts, the Admiralty will buy it in after a shipyard inspection."

"It is in good order, sir. My bos'n and carpenter climbed all round her below decks and she seems to be almost new."

"Good, good, Captain. Now then, I have orders for you. Both you and Mr Grahame here, are to travel to London to meet Admiral Sir David Edwards and Lord Stevenage with all despatch. I will send your reports to London by the courier who is to leave shortly. Meanwhile your ship will remain here for a dockyard inspection and re-supply but that could take three or four weeks as there are so many ships wanting attention, all supposed to be in desperate need because of the wear and tear of continual blockade duty. Your officers may go ashore and also parties of dependable men. You can start in the morning. My Lieutenant will give you your orders on the way out and I'll see you again when you return. So goodbye for now, gentlemen."

Chapter Three

Merriman hears of the League of Neutrality

On the steps of the Admiralty building Merriman paused, thinking about all that had happened here on his previous interviews. Each time he had been given a new ship and the last time he had been promoted to the rank of Post Captain.

"Come along, James, have you gone to sleep? We mustn't keep the gentlemen waiting," said Grahame, turning back from two steps higher where he had stopped on realising that Merriman was not keeping up with him.

"My apologies, sir, this place brings back such memories."

Once again they were shown into the big Admiralty room with the huge mahogany table in the centre. Merriman glanced at the wind indicator on one wall connected to the wind vane far above on the roof. Admiral Sir David Edwards rose to greet them and asked them to be seated.

"Good morning, gentlemen. It is a pleasure to see you again. You seem to have had an interesting time in India according to your report, Captain, which I received yesterday. Admiral Fitzherbert sent it by courier whilst you were travelling by the mail coach. I'm expecting Lord Stevenage to arrive very shortly and I know he is looking forward to seeing you both again."

They didn't have long to wait before the same harassed Lieutenant knocked and announced the arrival of Lord Stevenage, Merriman's patron. All stood to greet him, the man who had the ear of the Prime Minister William Pitt the younger. Merriman was shocked to see how much he had aged in the time since they last met. He had always had some grey hair and now it was almost completely white and many more lines creased his face.

Nevertheless he greeted them warmly, saying to Merriman, "I was deeply sorry to learn of the death of your mother and your father, James. When I attended your wedding I learned that your mother was ill and not expected to live long, but my cousin your father seemed fit for many more years. You have my condolences."

"And mine also, James. I remember your father well. We were young lieutenants together in the old Terror and good friends. I am sorry to hear that they have both gone," said the Admiral.

"Thank you both for that, gentlemen," replied Merriman. "I am hoping that I will have the opportunity whilst I am in England to see my wife and new son and sort out any problems my father may have left with the estate."

As he was speaking both Lord Stevenage and the Admiral smiled conspiratorially and then the Admiral said with a grin, "All taken care of, Captain. As you know your ship is to receive a thorough overhaul before you leave Portsmouth again which could take up to three weeks or more as they are so busy, so you are free to journey home in that time."

"Thank you, Sir David, that will be marve…"

He was interrupted by his Lordship saying, "There is more, James. I went to your father's funeral and told your wife, Helen, that if she had any problems to tell me as I know many good lawyers and I could send one of my bailiffs to help with the estate if needed. She replied, thanking me and saying that all seemed to be in order but you have many documents to sign. As you may well know I have been keeping a distant eye on your wife and estate. Helen wrote and told me that she was expecting a child and I wrote back to say that I would be honoured to be a godfather if she agreed, which she did. The child is not yet christened, she wanted you to be there, but it will happen as soon as you are home."

"Thank you, my Lord, thank you. I don't know what else to say. I'm taken all aback. Anyway, as soon as you have finished with me here I must go and arrange for a seat on the mail coach."

His Lordship smiled again. "As I am to go to your home for the christening, James, we can travel up there in my coach."

Poor Merriman was so excited by the news that his attention had to be brought back to matters in hand by a discreet cough from Admiral Edwards.

"Now, gentlemen, both his Lordship and I have studied your reports most keenly and we are of the same mind that you both have completed your orders far better than we expected. Your exploits have been most interesting. I am pleased to see that you captured two prizes, Indian frigates which the Honourable John Company has agreed to buy, although payment has still to be made. When it is, Captain, your share of the prize money will go into your account and their share apportioned to your officers and men. And not content with that," said the Admiral with a twinkle in his eye, "you collected a French corvette on your way home. Is there no end to your exploits? If it is sound the Admiralty will certainly buy it in and so you and your men will all receive their share. We are always short of frigates as you know and the French ships are well made, and of course there is head money due to you for the French prisoners. Oh, and the English sailors you rescued have been sorted out and when recovered will go to other ships."

"Yes, Sir David, I have already claimed some of them as replacements for the men I have lost in India, including a Master's Mate. So my ship is fully crewed except that I need another junior lieutenant and perhaps two more midshipmen. Of course it is possible I may lose one or two men if they choose to desert when at Portsmouth, but in the main they are all reliable men."

"Excellent, Captain, they will be waiting for you when you re-join your ship. Now perhaps, Your Lordship, you would care to enlighten these gentlemen about what has been happening here and what their next orders will involve."

"Thank you, Admiral. Well, the problem nearest to home that we have is the proposed treaty between the Russian Tsar, Paul, and Sweden, Denmark-Norway and Prussia, which they will call The League of Armed Neutrality. There was one some time ago and it quickly fell apart. Of course we and the Royal Navy have adopted a policy of unlimited searches of neutral vessels going into French ports in an attempt to cut off military supplies and other imports useful to the French Republic. Those countries naturally object to their ships being stopped as the aim of their treaty is to enforce free trade with France."

He paused to take a sip of water then continued, "This poses another difficulty as we need many of the exports from those countries ourselves, timber and other naval stores, hemp, canvas, pitch and all the rest, and if they agree to the treaty, as seems likely, it will cut our own supplies. The Government considers that this can be considered a hostile action and certain steps are being taken to stop it if we can. You will know that some of those countries have many warships, not as many as we do but if they joined together they would form a very serious threat. We propose to send a fleet to make a show of force there, with the intention of trying to detach Denmark from the League by diplomatic means or actual hostilities but it will be the beginning of next year before we can gather a strong enough force. Admiral, would you continue?"

"Thank you, my Lord. Later this year, Captain, your ship is to go into the North Sea taking Mr Grahame with you and it will be his task to visit our embassies and our people in each country to determine the development of the treaty. As usual, Captain, you are in command of the ship but also under the command of Mr Grahame who will decide where he wishes you to go. Is that clear to you, gentlemen? Good. Then you, Mr Grahame, will receive further instructions from your superiors and you, Captain, can go home to your family. A courier will bring your orders."

"My carriage will collect you at eight o'clock tomorrow morning, James, and I hope we have a trouble free journey," said Lord Stevenage. "Sir Edward has despatched a courier with documents to the north and a letter to your wife to tell her that you will soon be home. Two or three days should do it, depending on the state of the roads."

"Thank you, sir, I'll be ready."

"Oh and, Captain, take your second epaulette on board, right away," said the Admiral. "You look unbalanced without it."

"Aye-aye, sir," responded a very happy Merriman.

Chapter Four

Merriman home for his new son's Christening

Returning to the family home, Burton Manor situated in the county of Cheshire north west of the city of Chester, brought Merriman so many memories, though he also noticed changes. The house and small estate had been purchased many years ago by Joseph Merriman, Merriman's father, a retired and notable frigate captain himself, who had been very fortunate in the matter of prize money and a small inheritance.

It was a comfortable, late 17th century gentleman's residence with stabling and coach house and some of the servant's quarters properly concealed round the back of the main house. From the raised position of the house, there was a fine view over the wide estuary of the River Dee. The village duck pond was visible from the room Merriman used as a boy. On that pond he used to sail his model ships and fight imaginary sea battles, his imagination fed by the stirring tales told by his grandfather, old Elias Merriman, of wild deeds and terrible gales, of fights with pirates and savages under tropical skies, until his mind could foresee no other future than to be a naval officer.

At the sound of Lord Stevenage's coach wheels crunching on the gavel in front of the house, the door was flung open and there was Helen at the top of the stone steps. At the sight of her, more beautiful if possible than when he saw her last, Merriman's heart gave a great throb. He leapt out of the coach and bounded up the stairs to sweep her into his arms with no thought of His Lordship or the servants watching. They hugged and kissed for several minutes before Merriman remembered his manners. His Lordship was still standing by his coach with a broad smile on his face and, as he climbed the steps up to the door, Helen gave him a deep curtsey as did the female servants. The menservants bowed, all of them impressed by the presence of a real aristocrat with his coach bearing his coat of arms on the doors.

"You are most welcome, my Lord. Please come in for some refreshment." Helen led him into the largest reception room of the house where a log fire blazed in the hearth. Some candles had been lit but the room was almost as bright as day with sunlight pouring through the big windows.

James had no eyes for anything or anybody other than Helen but he was brought back to his duties as host by Helen's hand on his arm. "My apologies. My Lord, please take a seat." Both men waited until Helen sat and then they made themselves comfortable on chairs near the fire.

As they sat Lord Stevenage said, "It is a delight for my eyes to see you again, my dear. You are as lovely as ever. James, you lucky dog, there is no need to apologise. I was young once myself, and your meeting reminded me of my own wife's greetings in years past."

A footman bearing a big silver tray carried drinks round and the conversation flowed easily between them. "Where is our little boy, Helen?" asked Merriman. "And who is looking after him?"

"Fast asleep, James, I didn't want to wake him. Annie is looking after him like a mother hen."

"Annie was my mother's friend and housekeeper for many years, my Lord. You will remember the splendid feast she arranged for the wedding."

"Indeed I do, James. I have often thought about it and on our journey home Mr Grahame and I, and your French captive Moreau also, discussed it at length. I have been welcomed to many big country houses but, as I told your mother, in none of them was I made more welcome than in this house."

Just then there was a knock on the door and Annie came in carrying the little boy. She curtseyed to his Lordship and passed the child over to his mother.

"I'm glad to see you again, Annie," said Merriman. "You are well and enjoying looking after your small charge, I hope?"

"Oh yes, sir, I am, keeps me on my toes, sir. I'm only sorry that your mother never lived to see the little darling but if she can see him she will love him as we all do."

While she was speaking the two men came across the room to Helen to see the new arrival to the family. The child looked up at them curiously, then grinned and waved his arm around clutching a small, knitted toy.

"A fine strong son you have there, James. I wish him well," said His Lordship.

"Thank you, my Lord," murmured Merriman, taking the little boy carefully into his arms and looking down into two bright blue eyes.

"James, be careful. Don't hold him too tightly. He won't break but don't drop him," Helen whispered. "It is time for his feed so Annie will see to it."

Merriman was reluctant to let his little son go and cradled him a little longer before passing him over to Annie.

"Helen, what arrangements have you made for the christening? Who is coming and who is staying? Have you arranged for His Lordship's accommodation?"

"No, James, his Lordship told me in his letter that he had would take rooms at the White Lion inn in Chester, but I hope, sir, that you will join us for dinner this evening."

Over the meal, pronounced excellent by Lord Stevenage, Helen told them what arrangements had been made for the ceremony the day after tomorrow. The vicar had been told that her husband was home and the guests also been told. At last Lord Stevenage departed for Chester and James and Helen made their way slowly up to bed, passing the family portraits on the walls. Merriman paused to view them - his grandfather, old Admiral Elias Merriman, and his wife Henrietta, Lord Stevenage's aunt, his uncle Nathaniel who had fought and died with his regiment in the American War. New among the portraits was one of his mother, a very old lady, and one of his father as well, both painted after Merriman left for India and before his mother's death.

Once alone, the couple fell into each other's arms and were soon in bed, murmuring endearments and caressing one another. Helen had lost none of her enthusiasm for making love and they finally fell asleep as dawn was tentatively showing itself in the sky.

Chapter Five

Merriman's patron Lord Stevenage is Godfather

The next day, with the weather being kind to them, James and Helen rode round their estate, looking at the arable farms and those with more livestock. All was well, fields ploughed ready for the next year's crops, the cattle sleek and healthy but muddy and pigs fat and very muddy. The hedges were neatly laid and ditches free of growth and rubbish. They met the appropriately named Mr Hedges, the estate bailiff and, on seeing them, Hedges dragged off his cap and bowed.

"Mr Hedges, I am pleased with all I see, you are to be congratulated on your work," said Merriman. "But I think some changes have been made since I was last here."

"Yes, sir, there is a new tenant in the lower farm. Old farmer Brown was too old and couldn't maintain the buildings as he should so he had to go."

"And where did he go, you didn't just throw him and his wife out did you?" said a concerned Merriman.

"Oh no, sir, your lady wife had the rooms above the stables cleaned out and whitewashed for them and they seem to be quite content."

"I want to start a new flower garden and grow some vegetables as well, James," said Helen. "The old garden has been overgrown with weeds and brambles so much has had to be bought. I thought Mr Brown could help me with that and his wife is helping in the kitchen too."

"That was a kindly thought, my dear," remarked Merriman. I know Father always tried to find somewhere comfortable for his old staff to go."

He turned in his saddle to look at Hedges. "Mr Hedges, where did you get all your ideas from for the changes and improvements I see?"

"Well, sir, it was Mrs Merriman who helped me. She told me about things she had learnt in India and they have worked. We are getting an increase in the yield from the crops and she found new ways to get jobs done quicker. The estate records are up at the house, sir, your wife checks them regularly and with her inspections of the farms I have to be on my toes. Ma'am, I must tell you that young David Thomas from the west farm is recovering nicely, thanks to you and the good doctor."

"Very well done, my love," said James as they rode home. "I am impressed by how quickly you have learned everything."

"Well I had to, James. It wasn't long after I came here before I suspected that your accountant was recording false figures and money from rents was disappearing into his own pocket, so I promptly discharged him. With nobody else to do it I had to learn quickly. Fortunately my father taught me a lot about his own accounts and book-keeping."

"Oh blast it, Helen, I'm sorry. I forgot to ask after the good doctor, your father, and his sister, your aunt. How are they?"

"Father is quite well but my aunt died last winter so I insisted that he sold his house and move into our dower house to be nearer. Of course he has the same couple who looked after us to look after him so he is quite content and he loves to play with his new grandson. I hope you are pleased with what I have done, James."

"Of course I am, I'm sure I couldn't have found a better chatelaine in the whole of the country. I gather from Hedges' remarks that you and your father have been looking after the tenants on the estate."

"Yes, James, we have and all the servants too. Father was getting bored with having no doctoring to do and suggested that we did a regular tour of the estate to see if anybody needed his help. So we have been going round once a week to visit them all."

"That is excellent news, Helen. Now, let us go home, I am famished and looking forward to a meal and playing with our boy and then I must go and see my parents' graves."

The graves were in Burton churchyard, two simple headstones with names and dates and a brief note about his father's rank in the navy.

"I hope you like them, James," Helen said. "I didn't think they or you would want anything too elaborate, but I had a plaque made to put on the wall inside the church. That has more about them on it."

Merriman stood in silence with his head bowed for a few minutes before he said, "You have done well, my love. It is no more or less than they would have wanted."

The following day was the christening. They had decided to name the child Robert William Edward. William after Lord Stevenage, William D'Ablay. They were joined in the church by some of their family and friends and many people from the estate. As the proud parents stood at the font, they were joined by Lord Stevenage, the godfather, smiling all over his face.

The ceremony over, most people went their separate ways except for some family members. The only outsider remaining with the party was his Lordship who, after a fine meal, stood and proposed a toast to his godson and his parents. Other toasts followed and people began to disperse. Eventually the only people left were James and Helen, her father, Lord Stevenage and Annie holding little Robert. She only stayed with them for a few moments before taking the child for his supper and up to bed.

Relaxing before the fire, quietly watching the flickering flames and with the three men each with a large glass of claret, Lord Stevenage coughed and spoke. "James and Helen, I have come to a decision. I have been made so welcome in this house that I feel almost one of the family. I have no family of my own now with my wife and son both being dead. My daughter disappeared to America with some landless rogue and I haven't heard from her in nearly twenty years. You know, James, that your father and I were cousins meaning you are the nearest to a family that I have. So I will tell you that upon my death all my own estate and great house and a small house in London will pass to you, James, with a separate arrangement for my godson. My will has been drawn up and I will not change it."

The others sat there speechless with amazement and his Lordship continued, "Of course my title will not pass to you, James, and without a son of my own it becomes extinct."

"S-Sir, I don't know what to say. I certainly didn't expect this. Are you absolutely certain there is no other branch of your family to whom the title and estate should go? I owe you a great deal for my advancement in the Navy, sir, for your patronage, but this is overwhelming."

"Yes, I'm certain. I am getting older and feeling it so I want to be sure it all falls into good hands. Of course you could sell the estate, after all you have a fine estate here, but if you do I hope you will try to ensure it goes into deserving hands. My staff would stay on until you decide but I have made ample provision for them in my will. So there it is, James, and it is settled. Now, if you will call for my carriage, I must go back to my rooms at the White Lion ready for an early start for London."

And so he left with their profuse thanks ringing in his ears. Astonished at their good fortune, James and Helen lay awake for hours talking about Lord Stevenage's generosity and what it would mean for them.

The next two weeks passed rapidly. Merriman's family lawyer came with his father's will and they went through all the necessary papers until everything was signed and completed and Merriman was the undoubted owner of the estate. One day a mud-spattered naval courier arrived with Merriman's new orders and informing him to report to Admiral Fitzherbert in Portsmouth. When he told Helen that his all too brief time away from his duties was ending she burst into tears.

"Oh, James, it's too soon, you've only been home for just over two weeks. When will I see you again? Last time you were away for more than two years. You will miss seeing Robert growing up."

"Now, now, my love, compose yourself," said Merriman. "When we were married you knew that I would be away for months or years at a time. You will be safe here and with no money worries what with the revenue from the estate and the prize money I have earned. You can draw on that as needed. Now I must send a message to Chester to reserve a seat on tomorrow's mail-coach."

That night their lovemaking was as passionate as ever but Merriman had to go and it was with a heavy heart he left his wife and home behind him, although he knew that, when he reached his ship, he would be back in his other home.

Chapter Six

Back to Portsmouth. New fleet to attack Dunkirk

Finally the coach arrived at the Portsmouth dockyard and Merriman alighted with his luggage. He found a porter who carried the luggage down to the quayside. Eagerly he looked for his ship, the frigate *Lord Stevenage* but, with the harbour so crowded with shipping, he couldn't see her. Two watermen were trying to attract his attention. He picked one and the man eagerly climbed up to pass the luggage down to his mate in the boat. Merriman descended the wet stone steps to the boat and seated himself in the stern.

"Which ship, sir?" asked the man.

"A frigate - *Lord Stevenage*," replied Merriman. "But I can't see her."

"She's moored on't far side, sir, behind that big three decker yonder."

As the men pulled strongly across the harbour, Merriman breathed deeply of the smells that he had known nearly all his life. The sea of course as well as the multiplicity of aromas of tar, rope, new canvas, sawn timber and paint. It was almost like coming home, he thought, then guiltily remembered his wife was at his real home.

As the boat neared the side of his ship, and at the hail from an officer, he threw back his boat cloak to show one of his epaulettes. At his nod the boatman shouted, "*Lord Stevenage.*"

That reply indicated that the captain was coming aboard and he could hear shouts and the clattering of shoes as the sideparty hastily mustered to greet him with all the due ceremony so beloved by the Navy. Climbing aboard, he found the officers gathered with his First Lieutenant David Andrews in front.

"Welcome aboard, sir. I hope you had a good journey," he said touching his hat in salute.

"Thank you, David. The journey was tolerable but I'm glad to be back."

Merriman took a long look about him but he knew that he would find nothing wrong and the details of the overhaul would be in the dockyard report. Looking again at the group of his officers he noticed one new face, a lieutenant, and two small midshipmen trying to make themselves even smaller and insignificant behind the others. Lieutenant Andrews introduced the lieutenant as Mr Eric Bristow and the new midshipmen as Mr John Evans and Mr William Edwards.

"Very well, gentlemen, I will see you all in my cabin in ten minutes, when all my belongings are sorted out." Indeed as he spoke he could see a party of men and his cox'n Matthews swaying his boxes aboard with his servant Peters anxiously watching to take them below and unpack them.

Once below, he said, "Peters, I want my best uniform out of that case and made ready to wear at once before you unpack anything else. I must go ashore and report my arrival to Admiral Fitzherbert without delay."

"Aye-aye, sir. Right away, sir," replied the man, already opening the case and shaking his head at the inevitable creases in the uniform. "Needs some ironing and straightening, sir, but I can put it right in no time." He disappeared with it into his own quarters.

Merriman looked around the great cabin, his home for the next months or even years. Everything looked the same, the woodwork had been newly varnished and the furniture well-polished – the furniture, something was different. Then he spotted the new item in the corner, a beautiful mahogany wine cooler. He crossed the cabin to look closely at the card attached to it, opened it and read, "To my dear husband, with all my love and best wishes and hope for a speedy return".

Merriman realised that Helen must have sent it to the ship whilst he was still at home, how she managed it without him knowing was a mystery. Lost in thought, he was brought back to earth by the Marine guard knocking on the door and announcing, "First Lieutenant and Officers, sir."

"Come in, gentlemen, and try and find a seat."

With twelve of them including the Master and the Doctor, there were not enough chairs to go round, so the midshipmen found space in the corners whilst most of their betters took the chairs and the bench below the stern windows.

"I am pleased to see you all again and very pleased to see some new faces amongst us. Lieutenant Bristow, how long have you been aboard and do you know everybody?"

"Only three days, sir, but I know my way about and the date of my commission means that I am to be your Third Officer."

"Very good, Mr Bristow, I look forward to knowing more about you soon. Mr Small, this means that you will continue to be Acting Fourth and still the senior Midshipman. Mr Green will take care of the signals, but I'm sure your turn will come if you continue your studies. And what about you two, Evans and Edwards, how long have you been aboard?"

Both of them shuffled their feet and flushed, the pair of them clearly feeling less than nothing on being addressed by their Captain. Evans recovered first and said, "We came aboard together, sir, only yesterday." Edwards nodded vigorously in agreement.

"Good, I will speak to you both later, meanwhile I hope Mr Small has found you your place below and that you will be eager to learn your duties. Now both of you may go." When the boys had left the cabin, Merriman said, "Gentlemen, I have to go ashore immediately to report to the Admiral and to collect our new orders, so I will tell you all later what those orders are. Is the ship fully stored and ready to leave, Mr Andrews? Good. Oh, and have my boat made ready."

As soon as they had left the cabin, Peters re-appeared with Merriman's best uniform pressed and clean, his hat knocked back into shape and with a clean shirt and necktie, breeches and stockings ready to put on. In moments Merriman changed with Peters fussing round him like an old mother hen.

"Damn it, I can manage man, leave me alone. I can fasten my own buttons," Merriman said testily. "And where are my other shoes?"

"Here, sir, I kept them polished and all your clothes clean and pressed while you were away, sir," said Peters in an aggrieved tone of voice.

"Of course, I knew you would. I'm sorry I swore at you."

Merriman left his cabin, carefully put his hat on and climbed up the companionway onto the deck. As he emerged into the fresh air he couldn't help automatically looking round again to see if he could find a fault but of course there was none. The side party of marines and the Bos'n and his mates and sideboys were ready to provide the usual ceremony due to a captain leaving his ship and the First Lieutenant and Lieutenant Bristow and others were standing waiting.

He climbed down into the boat where all the men were dressed in their special outfits and Matthews, his cox'n, was at the stern with the tiller.

"Glad to see you with both epaulettes, sir," Matthews whispered as Merriman sat down.

Merriman merely grunted, his mind fully occupied by the coming meeting with the Admiral. He was not kept waiting long and Admiral Fitzherbert welcomed him warmly.

"Pleasure to see you again, Captain. I hope your time at home was all you hoped for?" Without waiting for a reply he went on, "I know your ship is all ready for sea again, the overhaul and repairs completed two days ago and I have seen new stores being swayed aboard. Your Lieutenant Andrews has overseen it all. Good man that, what?"

"Yes, sir, he is. I could wish for none better. When the time comes to take command of his own ship I shall be sorry to lose him. He has been with me since he was a midshipman."

"Yes, I've seen his record and he is due for promotion when a ship becomes available. Now then, Captain, you asked Admiral Edwards for a new Lieutenant and two new midshipmen. They are aboard and I can only hope they prove better than my nephew was."

He was referring to the time a few years ago when he had asked Merriman to take his nephew as midshipman. The seventeen year old had proved useless, indeed he turned out to be a depraved character and a murderer. Merriman had shot him after he had killed four marines.

"Indeed, sir, I have met them and I'll sort them out."

"Well, Merriman, here are your new orders posted from London. You are off to the North Sea, I believe, later this year, with your friend Mr Grahame. But I have been told that he will not be here for several weeks yet. Off on some busy spy hunting somewhere, I suppose. Meanwhile, you will join a small force gathering to attack Dunkirk where we know the French have gathered together a squadron of four frigates which escape when they can to destroy British coastal shipping. Of course the biggest ports are blockaded by our ships of the line but we don't have enough ships to blockade all the small ports completely, so this forthcoming attack has been ordered by their Lordships of the Admiralty."

Merriman nodded and the Admiral went on, "Captain Henry Inman of the frigate *HMS Andromeda* will be in command of the force being put together including *HMS Nemesis*, the sloop *HMS Dart* and numerous smaller vessels which include four fireships. The force is nearly all assembled so Captain Inman will be calling all captains to his ship tomorrow morning to meet you and explain his proposals for the attack. You will come back here after the attack to collect Mr Grahame who should be here by then. Is all of that clear, Captain? Your orders will be given to you on your way out. Good luck to you, sir."

Back on board the *Lord Stevenage* Merriman found his clerk Tomkins arranging documents on the desk for his signature. These were reports from all departments of the ship from the Bos'n to the Gunner, the Carpenter, the Purser and others regarding the contents of the store rooms and the condition of the various stores, food and water, powder and shot, spare cordage and canvas in them and all the other hundreds and hundreds of other things needed to keep a ship of war ready for anything, especially as the ship could be far from a friendly dockyard and had to be self-sufficient.

Merriman knew that Tomkins was assiduous in checking all the reports, going below to check every total before bringing it to his captain. In fact he had a running battle with the purser, a man named Grummage. As the purser was not paid by the Admiralty, it was expected that the purser on every ship would make his own income and try to feather his own nest by recording a lower amount of rum, the slop chest containing spare clothes for the crew, and as many other items he could sell to the crew at a profit. Tomkins had found many discrepancies in the purser's totals and reported them to the captain. This had the result that the man had received a severe reprimand - not for the first time - from Merriman who had tried to find a replacement for the man, but without success.

Merriman knew he could trust Tomkins so he signed the papers without delay. Tomkins had been a seaman aboard the flagship *Queen Charlotte* and was severely injured in the battle off Ushant called The Glorious First of June. When Merriman was a midshipman, Tomkins had saved him from a severe fall from aloft so, when he found the man begging outside the Admiralty, he had promised him a berth on the *Lord Stevenage*. Tomkins was not fit for active or heavy duties but when he told Merriman that he could read and write and do sums, he quickly became an ideal captain's clerk. "Old Miss Dawkins beat all that into us with 'er cane, sir," he had said.

Up on deck again. Merriman announced to his officers that in half an hour he was going to do a Captain's Inspection of every part of the ship. The delay meant that all members of the ship's company had a last chance to put anything right that needed it before the captain found it. From experience they knew that Merriman never missed a thing, so there was an instant bustle as they tried to ensure that everything was in order. He went below to change out of his best uniform into his normal seagoing rig, more suitable for visiting every part of his ship.

The first lieutenant was waiting for him, touched his hat and reported, "All ready for inspection, sir."

"Very good, Lieutenant, but tell me what the dockyard did to the ship. Amongst all the reports I found nothing from them."

"No, sir, I have asked them repeatedly for their complete report but there is nothing yet. They did a good job of it though, new standing and running rigging, some new copper plates below and they did more thorough repairs than the carpenter was able to do at sea. We have been given two new eighteen pounder guns to replace two that were considered too worn to be used much longer and you will have seen the two extra smashers on the foredeck, I'm sure. Everything has been repainted and the decks cleaned of the rubbish that the dockyard people left behind, sir. I hope you will be pleased. They will have seen you come aboard and maybe that will speed up their report. The only problem we have is cleaning the deck under the pens where we keep the pigs and hens you sent aboard. An ideal punishment for any defaulter, I think."

"Maybe, David, maybe. After I have inspected the ship I will have go ashore again and see what I can do about that report. So now let us be about it."

Merriman went through the ship from stem to stern below followed by the various responsible people and then up to the gundeck where the men were standing to their guns. There, using his telescope, he inspected the new rigging. He found little wrong however, small things such as one of the hammocks in the nettings not rolled tightly enough and one gun carriage wheel needing some repair which had been disguised by paint. He returned on deck to find a worried man from the dockyard waiting for him with the tardy report. Merriman scowled at him and took him below to wait whilst he read it.

"Thank you, that seems to be complete," he said finally. "You have done a good job, except for a wheel on one of the guns which needs replacing. If you will send some men to fix it right away I will then sign your report and send it back to you."

"Thank you, sir. I'm sure you will find everything done satisfactorily, your officers checked everything as we did it."

Merriman dismissed the man with a nod, reminding him that the wheel should be dealt with immediately. Only then did he sit down to read his orders from the Admiralty in detail. He was to be ready to leave as soon as Captain Inman arranged it, with Inman to explain exactly what was expected of them all.

Chapter Seven

French ships attacked in Dunkirk harbour

All was ready by the 17th of June but, for ten days, adverse winds and tides prevented the operation starting. When the squadron arrived off Dunkirk they realised that the French were expecting them. They had anchored their frigates in a line across the harbour from east to west, with gunboats patrolling the harbour. Some of the French frigates could make their escape into channels in the Braak Sands if too hard pressed, where Inman's ships dare not follow. Captain Inman knew that his biggest ships *Andromeda*, *Nemesis* and *Lord Stevenage* drew too much water and could even be a liability in the narrow harbour.

He sent orders for all three to wait offshore and disperse some of their crews into the smaller ships. The attack was led by the *Dart* under Commander Campbell with the other ships that would lead the attack being followed the fireships *HMS Wasp*, *Comet*, *Falcon* and *Rosario* followed by two brigs, the *Biter* and *Boxer*, and other ships. The squadron approached the harbour in the late evening in line ahead with *Dart* leading. Some of the ships had men aboard pressed from smuggling vessels, so they were able to act as guides among the sandbanks as they neared the harbour.

Merriman and his officers watched what followed with keen anticipation. *HMS Dart* was unusual in that she was heavily armed with thirty 32-pounder carronades to a new design which were faster to reload. The sloop quietly passed the French ships until she was level with the last frigate but one. Alerted by something, that ship opened fire. Campbell responded, knowing his heavy carronades were devastating at close range and had ordered them to be double shotted. Therefore each gun carried double the ordinary number of missiles and the casualties and severe damage wreaked before the frigate could reply meant that the sloop was past and firing again and again into the last frigate in the line, the *Desiree'*.

In the darkness it was difficult for the watchers outside the harbour to see exactly what was going on but the repeated flashing of cannon fire gave some indication of events.

"I'd like to be there, sir," said Shrigley. "I can't see it but I expect our ships are firing twice to the enemies' once and look there, sir, the fireships are attacking the other end of the line."

Merriman studied what the fireships were doing and then suddenly exclaimed, "The French were expecting that and three of them have slipped their anchor cables and are sailing into the channels in the sandbanks."

"Surely our ships are shooting at them, sir?" asked Midshipman Green.

"Indeed they are, Mr Green, and doubtless causing much damage, especially the carronades on the *Dart,* but they have reached the main channel to the harbour, I think."

Merriman turned his attention to the four blazing fireships. Abandoned by their crews they were drifting aimlessly until one by one they exploded without causing the results hoped for.

Meantime Commander Campbell in *HMS Dart* had been busy. He laid his ship alongside the *Desiree'* and, after hard hand-to-hand fighting, the ship was captured. Merriman, and all who could, had been following these events as well as they could in the darkness but it was not until a lookout aloft hailed, "Deck there, I think *Dart* has captured one of the frigates, sir. It's leaving the line and moving to sea."

Cheering broke out from the crew with excited chattering. Merriman felt like joining in but he remembered in time that he should not show his feelings openly, a captain should hold himself aloof.

"Well, gentlemen," he said eventually. "It appears to be over."

Sure enough the flashes and thunder of cannon fire had died down to almost nothing and the British ships were withdrawing. In the darkness it was hard to be sure but all seemed to be safe, though probably damaged to some extent.

"That will show the Frogs who is master, sir. They can't hide from the Navy," said Lieutenant Andrews. "It's a pity we couldn't do more than lend some of our men to strengthen the crews. We have been useless out here, sir."

"Not exactly useless, David," replied Merriman. "We are here to stop any of the French from escaping, and anyway I think you will get your fill of fighting. We haven't finished with Bonaparte yet."

The fifty men lent to the other ships returned full of tales of their experiences, chattering to their mates until Merriman said to the officer of the watch, "I'll have the deck cleared, Mr Merryweather. It's like being in a crowd of washerwomen."

Eventually the squadron re-assembled out at sea and Captain Inman sent *Lord Stevenage* back to Portsmouth with his reports. The captured frigate was already nearly there.

Reporting to Admiral Fitzherbert, Merriman was told that Mr Grahame was waiting for him ashore and a messenger would be sent to find him.

"When he is back on board, Captain, your earlier orders will take effect and you will sail for the North Sea," the Admiral said.

Chapter Eight

Sailing to the Baltic

The early light of dawn found the *Lord Stevenage* on the larboard tack, heading down the Solent and Spithead. There there was a good deep water anchorage, well-sheltered from winds except from the southeast. They took the easterly exit to the English Channel and left the Isle of Wight to starboard. Of course Spithead was where the infamous Spithead Mutiny took place in 1797.

Mr Grahame had come aboard late last night and so, as soon as there was enough light to see the signal from the Admiral to set sail, there was immediate bustle as the men dashed to their places. All had gone well and, as the first rollers began to be felt beneath the ship, Merriman saw the Bos'n checking the tension of the refitted shrouds, the main ropes holding the masts up. They were all new and he knew that they would be expected to stretch at sea and would have to be tightened up several times, as would the forestays and backstays.

Merriman had watched keenly the actions of the few new men sent to his ship and was pleased to see that they were all experienced seamen. The new lieutenant was watching everything closely and the two new midshipmen were wisely keeping out of the way, looking wide eyed at all that was happening around them. As the ship moved out into the Channel, they were already at action stations, after all the country was at war with France and who knew but that they would encounter some venturesome Frenchman close inshore. However, they saw no French ships only small English coasters as they turned east so action stations were unnecessary.

Merriman turned to the officer of the watch and said, "The ship is yours, Lieutenant Merryweather."

He went below and Peters, his servant, arrived in the cabin a few moments later. Long experience told him that the captain would want to shave and change his clothes before breakfast and he would also be hungry. Peters had everything ready. The cook's assistant arrived with a big jug of warm water and Merriman was washed and shaved very quickly. As he finished dressing, the cook's boy arrived with his breakfast. At this stage of things, there was fairly fresh bread with butter from a tub kept below, bacon and eggs, and a big jug of fresh coffee.

As Merriman expected, a rather bleary-eyed Grahame put in an appearance. He sniffed the air and said, "Good morning, James. I'm sure the smell of that coffee woke me up and I'm ravenous. What have you got for me, Peters?"

"The same as the captain, sir - bacon, eggs and bread and butter. I'll fetch it right away." He poured out some coffee for Grahame and fled.

As they finished their leisurely breakfast, the men discussed the details of their next task. "It's really much the same as we did in Ireland, the West Indies and in India, James. I will tell you where I have to go to find our agents. You will take me there and I will go ashore."

"Very well, sir. We have good charts of the Danish and Norwegian coasts and I foresee no difficulty about that. My officers do not yet know where we are going so I am proposing, with your permission, to invite some of them to dinner this evening so that we can tell them what our orders are."

"Let us do that then, James. Now I'm off to my cot again to try and catch up with some sleep, it has been a busy few days for me and I have missed a lot."

And so Merriman invited Lieutenants Andrews, Shrigley, and Bristow, the Marine Captain Edward St James, one of the two new midshipmen and the Sailing Master Mr Henderson as well as Mr Grahame and the doctor to join him in the great cabin. A pleasant evening ensued. The meal was served by Peters, helped by Tomkins. Merriman had ordered the cook to slaughter one of his pigs and the cabin was filled with the aroma of roast pork. Edwards, the midshipman, still only thirteen years old and somewhat abashed in the company of his seniors, nevertheless managed to eat a huge meal and, fortified by a glass of good claret, made a reasonable attempt at proposing the Loyal Toast.

The table was cleared and then Peters served coffee and some of Merriman's best brandy.

All were relaxed and full of good food when Merriman said, "Gentlemen, Mr Grahame and I wish to tell you what this commission is all about, so listen carefully." He rapped on the table and said loudly, "Mr Edwards, if you will kindly keep awake, you will learn something."

The boy, well fed and under the influence of the claret, had been struggling to keep his eyes open and was almost asleep but quickly recovered to find all the rest of the assembly watching him. "S-sorry, sir," said the embarrassed and red-faced midshipman. "It's a long time since I enjoyed such a good meal, sir. A midshipman doesn't get the chance very often."

Lieutenant Shrigley was grinning all over his face and Merriman said, "It is not so very long ago that you could eat like that, Alfred. You had a prodigious appetite when you were a midshipman, as I recall. I remember one occasion, gentlemen, when our Mr Midshipman Shrigley fell into the hold of a fishing boat, he was so eager to find fish for his tea. He emerged covered in fish scales."

All roared with laughter and Shrigley, by now well used to being teased about the incident, merely smiled weakly and said, "You all know that I was pushed by one of the fishermen."

Merriman brought the hilarity to an end by saying, "Gentlemen, down to business. What we are to do is much the same as we have done before in Ireland and India - to put Mr Grahame ashore where he needs to go to try to contact our agents and Embassy people in Denmark-Norway and Sweden. Perhaps you would care to amplify my remarks, sir?" He turned to Grahame.

"Thank you, Captain," he said and he proceeded to recount to them all that was known about the League of Armed Neutrality and what it would mean for Britain. "I'll leave it to you, Captain, to discuss the naval preparations."

Merriman began, "The Admiralty is proposing to put a squadron together to sail to the Baltic and Copenhagen with a view of persuading those countries, by diplomacy if possible and force if necessary, to abandon the whole idea of the League. As you will know, gentlemen, the Channel Fleet under Earl St Vincent has to cover the whole East coast and South coast of our island, down through Biscay and the French coast and Spain. It is a huge area and it will be difficult to spare enough ships from there or anywhere else to form another fleet. It could be early next year before enough are assembled. Meanwhile we are to take Mr Grahame wherever he wishes to go and then report back home with any information he may collect. Any questions, gentlemen?"

"Are we likely to form part of that squadron, sir?" asked Lieutenant Bristow.

"We have no orders to that effect as yet but I certainly hope so," replied Merriman.

Conversation continued for a while then the party broke up for some of them were needed on deck for the change of Watch.

Chapter Nine

Trouble at Merriman's home

A very upset Helen was sitting in front of her mirror while her maid Jennifer combed her hair for her. She was sure that she was pregnant again and must write to James to tell him, although she knew that it could take months for her letter to reach him, maybe not until after the baby was born. And should she tell him about the villains who had attacked her? It would only worry him and doubtless he had enough to worry about without that, so she decided not to.

She went over the events again in her mind. She had been returning home after visiting one of the estate farms. The coachman was ill and so her small carriage was being driven by one of the experienced stable hands by the name of George. As they approached the gate onto the driveway up to the Manor, she saw three rough-looking men standing there, one of whom grabbed one of the two horses' bridles to stop it. One of the other two men reached for the carriage door, saying to his mate, "We've got a live one 'ere, Joe, wotcher fink we should do wiv 'er?"

He got no further. With his whip her driver laid open the cheek of the man holding the horse who screamed and staggered back, releasing his grip. With the second blow of his whip, George struck one of the other two men who cowered away from the blow. George then cracked his whip over the heads of the horses and they bolted, leaving the men behind. One of them was shouting something about getting even with her and the boy but then they were out of earshot.

Nearing the house George drew the horses back to a walk and pulled them into the stableyard. Another man came forward to help Helen down and she turned to George and said, "Thank you, George, you did well. Without your quick thinking who knows what those fellows might have done. I'll not forget what you did."

Not until she reached her own room did the reaction set in. She dropped into a chair, weeping and trembling violently. A frightened Jennifer tried to console her but without success, so she ran off to fetch Annie the housekeeper.

The motherly figure of Annie quickly managed to calm Helen down and soon she managed to give them a coherent account of what had happened. They were horrified, asking questions in a babble before she quietened them. "I'll come down when I have changed and washed so you, Jennifer, can help me while you, Annie, have a stable boy ride to fetch Mr Hedges here. But don't use the main gateway. When he is here, please have all the servants gathered together and I will speak to them."

When all were gathered together, she told them what had happened and what they must do.

"We must be on our guard, especially overnight. Those men threatened to get even so it may be just idle threats in anger or worse. Mr Hedges, if you will ride round the estate and warn every one of our tenants that there are villains about and to be on their guard. You could also call at the Dower house and ask my father to bring his pistols and the two servants here right away. Those men attacked me and so all the womenfolk must be kept close. Most of the men will have muskets or fowling pieces so they should keep them loaded and handy. Those of you who live in the stable buildings must keep a watch out in turns and keep the gates to the stableyard locked and bolted."

"Yes, ma'am, we can do that. I'm an old soldier so I can organise that but we've only got my old fowling piece between us," said old farmer Brown. "Although we have pitchforks and clubs," he added thoughtfully. "If they try anything round the stables we can give them a warm welcome."

"Very well, Mr Brown. We have a few muskets in the house so you can have two of them. In the house we can secure all the doors and shutters tonight and keep watch in turns. Can anyone else use a firearm?" she asked.

"Aye, ma'am, I can," answered a footman, Edwin by name, "and so can Will here. We were both seamen aboard old Captain

Merriman's last ship, ma'am. When he retired he brought us here with him. I was his cox'n."

"Good. Edwin, you take charge of all the pistols in the house. I know there are several so have them all loaded and then each man can keep a loaded weapon ready. I have my own upstairs so I too will be ready." She turned to the maids and kitchen staff. "You can help by being ready to provide food for the men on watch, but all of you people remember, there are villains about. We saw only three but there could be more."

And so it was settled. The house bedded down for the night with lanterns placed in suitable positions so that the guards could see. Helen lay awake for some time before dropping off to sleep, wondering if there was anything else she could have done except for sending a man to warn the magistrates which she would do as soon as it got light enough in the morning.

She was woken by the noise of splintering wood and breaking glass downstairs and then gunshots. Quickly rising, she threw on a robe and seized her pistols from the bedside table and cocked them. Hardly had she done so when she heard a scream from her maid outside and then the door to her bedroom was flung violently open and her attacker from earlier appeared. He grinned when he saw her standing there holding the pistols and said with a leer, "Pistols, eh? A woman doesn't know pistols. I bet they ain't even loaded." He stepped towards her.

With no hesitation, she raised one of her pistols and fired at him. The ball hit his shoulder and threw him back but he quickly recovered and lunged for her again. Again she fired, and this time there was no mistake, the ball hit him in the chest and he collapsed, bleeding over the floor.

She rapidly reloaded her pistols, mentally thanking her husband for his insistence that she learned to shoot. Ready, she looked out into the balcony overlooking the hallway and saw three roughly-dressed men kneeling with their hands clasped behind their heads and threatened by Edwin and Will with pistols. Two women and a houseboy were in one corner and Annie was trying with shaking hands to load a pistol. Two other men were on the floor in the huddled attitudes of death with her father checking that they were indeed dead. Then gunshots and screams were heard from behind the house where the stables were. Obviously there were more villains than the six in the house and they were attempting to get into the stables.

Edwin shouted to the women, "There is rope in one of the store rooms. Fetch it here and we can tie these men up, quickly now."

The women disappeared into the back of the house as Helen came down the wide stairway into the hall. "Have any of our people been hurt?" she asked her father.

"Nothing serious in the house, Helen, but of course I don't know what is happening outside. I heard shots from upstairs, what happened there and are you alright?"

"One of them, I think the leader, broke in through a window in a room up there but I shot him. I think he is dead."

The women appeared with several coils of rope and, while Will kept his pistol ready, Edwin turned one of the bodies over and removed a knife buried in the man's chest. He wiped the blade on the man's clothing before taking up the rope and cutting it into pieces. Helen was amazed at how quickly the knife cut it but then she remembered it was a seaman's knife, always ready and sharp, though she had not seen him wearing it before. He tied the three men up with typical naval thoroughness using knots that they would never be able to get free from, then he turned to Helen and said, "Would you like me to go and see what has happened at the stables, ma'am?"

She was just about to reply when a gunshot sounded and a pistol ball barely missed her and thudded into the body of one of the tied men. Without a pause both Edwin and Will spun round and fired as one at the figure leaning over the railing at the head of the stairs. It was the man that Helen thought was dead and he was thrown backwards by both balls that hit him and then he bounced off the wall behind him and crashed over the railing and down on to the hall floor. This time there was no mistake, he was dead.

The men left to find out what had happened outside but were soon back. "All's well, ma'am," reported Edwin. "They tried to get into the stables but your people there shot two of them dead and overpowered another one. He is safely tied up but they tell me that they think there were two more that got away but one of those is certainly wounded."

Two men from the stables appeared pushing their captive ahead of them. One was the ex-soldier Brown and the other George, the stable boy, who was prodding the captive with a pitchfork.

It was all over. Helen sat down with a bump on one of the hall chairs, her legs trembling too much to stand but this time with relief. Edwin appeared in front of her and said, "Ma'am, we have four men prisoners and five men dead and two escaped. That is eleven of them, ma'am. If you hadn't prepared us so well some of us would be lying there instead. We have you to thank for our victory."

She nodded, taking control again. "Thank you, Edwin, and thank you all. Now get these bodies out of here and have the prisoners put somewhere secure. You girls, get some hot water and clean up the mess here and also in my bedroom. Father, will you come upstairs to see what happened to Jennifer, my maid. I heard her scream before that man burst into my room but what happened to her I don't know."

The girl was alive but nursing a badly bruised face. The doctor examined her and announced, "She has received a bad blow but nothing seems to be broken. Her bruises will heal in due course but she should rest."

Once the bodies had been removed and the blood cleaned up, Helen asked all the men into the big room and offered them all a glass of brandy which they accepted instantly. "Thank you all, gentlemen, for what you have done. I will ensure that Captain Merriman hears about it in due course. George, I want you to ride in the morning to the magistrate in Neston and report all of this. He will send some men to take the prisoners off our hands. The dead can be buried but not before he has seen them. Meanwhile I think one or two of you should keep watch until daylight and then we can have the windows and shutters repaired."

Chapter Ten

Capture of brig running arms to France

A few days after the Dunkirk raid, the *Lord Stevenage* was far past the south coast of England and well out into the North Sea heading north-east. The weather was fair although wisps of fog were still clearing slowly under the sun's warmth. Merriman stood on deck, looking keenly about him. All seemed to be in order with seamen busy cleaning everything. Even the rack of leathern fire buckets glowed, well-polished. The bos'n and a party of men were tightening the new shrouds on the lee side and the ship's master, Tom Henderson, was instructing the two new midshipmen whilst keeping an eye on his mates on the big wheel.

Merriman walked over and stood watching for a moment before asking, "Mr Henderson, how are these two young men doing?"

"Well, they seem keen to learn, sir, but they have a lot to learn. I decided to teach these new lads separately from the two older boys who already have a good knowledge of navigation and seamanship, sir. They'll soon be ready for their Lieutenant's Examination when they are old enough."

"Good idea, Mr Henderson, and how do you find your new master's mate, Mr Sorenson?"

"He's a good man, sir. I would have no fears about leaving him in charge. I think he would be well able to teach these youngsters while I concentrate on the older two, sir, with your approval of course, sir."

"Very well, Mr Henderson, make it so. You two boys must remember all that Mr Henderson and Mr Sorenson tell you and remember also the old saying 'knowledge is a treasure but practice is the key to it'."

Both of the young midshipmen were looking at him with flushed faces, doubtless promising themselves to do the best they could.

At that moment Grahame appeared on deck and saw Merriman at his usual exercise, walking up and down in his 'quarter deck walk', avoiding by instinct the numerous ringbolts and other impedimenta on the deck. "And how are you this fine morning, James?"

"Well enough, sir, have you determined where we are to go first?"

"Yes I have, perhaps we should adjourn to your cabin to discuss it."

Down below, seated and with coffee supplied by Peters, Grahame began, "I have determined to go straight for Copenhagen to the British embassy there. We are not exactly on the best of terms with Denmark-Holland or Sweden but as we are not yet at war it should be safe enough. It might be wise for you to arrange to purchase something from the dockyard there as an excuse for our presence, fresh water perhaps or something else needed for a ship. While I am ashore it would be a good opportunity for you to make a note of the defences there and plot them on your chart. That would be very useful if we have to attack there. Count the number of ships there of all kinds and look for any signs of new earth works for cannon and the disposition of the forts, but, and I stress but, do not go ashore, just note what you can see from the ship. I am accredited as a diplomat so I should have no difficulty reaching the embassy. How long I shall be I don't know but stay at anchor until I return, though be ready to sail at a moment's notice."

"That should be easy enough, sir, but if my ship is fired upon or any hostile moves made I must move away. I think the best thing for me to do is to start some water casks and take them ashore for refilling. That may give us a closer look into the dockyard."

"Good, James, that is what we will do. Do you think it will take more than a few days to get there?"

"Normally no, sir, but you may have noticed that the wind is dropping and that will slow the ship down. Also, we may encounter more mist or fog which is quite common at this time of year."

The next morning, Merriman was wakened by the duty midshipman, Evans. "Lieutenant Shrigley's compliments, sir, but we have run into thick fog and he has ordered Action Stations, sir, very quietly."

"Very well, thank you. I'll come up," replied Merriman.

It was a thick fog and it was hard to see anything beyond a few yards but Merriman knew that any number of ships could be close by.

"I'll have extra lookouts aloft, Mr Shrigley, and more ahead," he said, "and keep the men at their stations for now. Can't take chances, you know."

Half an hour later, though nothing was seen from the deck, a masthead lookout, also barely seen from the deck, hailed, "Deck there, I can see a ship's masts, sir, sticking up out of the fog to starboard."

"Send another man up there with a telescope if you please, Mr Shrigley, maybe he can see more."

The man was soon back. "It's a brig, sir, or a small sloop, only two masts but we can see only the top of them, sir."

"Well done, now go back aloft and report anything you see when the fog lifts."

"Aye-aye, sir," the man said and ran up the shrouds like a monkey.

Merriman thought for a few moments then ordered a slight change of course to starboard to gradually close with the other ship. There had been little wind for the past few hours but suddenly a strong breeze sprang up from the south-east. The *Lord Stevenage's* sails filled and she surged ahead. The fog quickly began to lift and revealed the other ship which, even as they watched, set more sail and turned to starboard.

"I recognise that ship, sir," said Shrigley. "She left Portsmouth the day before we did. Can't mistake her, sir, her main tops'l is a different colour and probably cleaner than the others."

Merriman immediately ordered one of the big bow-chasers to be loaded and be ready to fire a warning shot ahead of the brig. "Mr Merryweather, have a boarding party told off and a boat ready. You will board her as soon as she stops and take Mr Goodwin and some marines with you."

The gun fired and the ball splashed into the sea ahead of the brig which took no notice of it and stubbornly continued on her course.

"Another shot, Mr Shrigley, if you please."

Again the other ship ignored the splash and continued on its way. Merriman thought about it. The brig could be a neutral Danish or Swedish ship and to fire into her could bring about the sort of incident that would bring about the war they hoped to avoid, but…

He made up his mind, saying, "Bring her level with the brig, Mr Henderson, but only two hundred yards away, and reduce sail to keep us alongside."

As the *Lord Stevenage* drew level, Merriman ordered the portlids lifted and the starboard guns run out to show the ship's teeth. That was too much for the captain of the brig and he ordered his crew to drop the sails. The boarding party was soon alongside and climbing on deck to face the sullen crew, eight men and the captain who was swearing and practically dancing about with rage. Lieutenant Merryweather was used to that kind of behaviour and waited until the man ran out of breath before asking where the ship was bound and what her cargo was.

That provoked a further blast of swearing and shouting amongst which Merryweather could pick out words such as 'Bloody pirates' and 'Heathen British Navy think they own the sea' and indeed swearing such as the lieutenant had not heard before. Becoming conscious that the English sailors and marines were grinning at him the man quietened down and Merryweather repeated his questions.

"None of your damned bloody business. The sea is free to all traders so why should I tell you what we are doing, damn you. It's my ship and I'll go anywhere and carry whatever I want to, so clear off and take your pansy crew with you."

That finally roused Merryweather who said, "If that's the way you want it, Captain…"

He ordered some of his men to open the hatches to inspect the cargo whilst others kept a close watch on the crew.

The hatch covers were soon off and one of his men shouted, "Lieutenant, sir, I think you'll want to see this."

Merryweather looked down to see new boxes of muskets, bayonets, and field guns with their wheels removed, kegs of powder and boxes and boxes of shot. Some of the boxes were marked in English and what Merryweather thought might be the Dutch language or some such. Amazed he turned to Lieutenant Goodwin of the marines. "Mr Goodwin, have your sergeant keep all these men under close guard. If anyone objects or argues you have my permission to shoot them and that includes the captain."

"Aye-aye, sir," was the reply and Goodwin ordered his men to make the prisoners sit down with their hands on their heads, including the captain.

Merryweather went down to the captain's cabin with Goodwin to look for any papers or documents that would help to explain the cargo and for whom it was intended. He found nothing immediately but then he looked into a low cupboard under the captain's bunk. Inside he saw and dragged out a leather wallet full of papers. Together they scrutinised the papers, most routine and expected - crew list, the watch-bill, and a bill of lading showing that the cargo had been loaded in Boston, plus the captain's log of daily details of the voyage. Under everything was a sealed envelope addressed in French.

Thinking quickly, Merryweather said, "I must take these to Captain Merriman right away. Take command, Mr Goodwin, see if you can find any Frenchmen amongst the crew. You have some good seamen in your party who can deal with any problems with the ship."

Back on board *Lord Stevenage*, the lieutenant showed the documents to Merriman who immediately ushered him below and called for Mr Grahame to join them in the great cabin.

"Mr Grahame, it seems that we have stumbled upon something that will interest you." He had Merryweather recount all the details of what he had found, the cargo and the documents and then he showed the sealed envelope to Grahame. "This is addressed in French, sir. Perhaps you would like to open it, and maybe it will tell us something which may be more to your interest."

Grahame slit the envelope open, glanced at the contents and then exclaimed, "By all the gods, James, this is amazing. We must study it closely. It is a report about Portsmouth harbour, our ship movements and even tells of the Admiralty plans for a fleet to assemble to go to the Baltic although those plans are far from finalised."

"Very well, sir. Lieutenant, you have done well. When this is all over I will require a full report. Now go back to the brig, your orders will follow when we have decided what to do with it."

"Aye-aye, sir," was the reply and Merryweather left.

"What I can gather from all these papers, James, is this. That ship loaded its cargo in Boston, bound for Europe somewhere, probably somewhere in the Netherlands which is now occupied by Napoleon's army. We must squeeze as much information as we can on that from the captain. This French report with all the information it contains can only be the result of a spy's activities round Portsmouth and the dockyard and even in London at the Admiralty."

"A spy in the dockyards and Admiralty? That is hard to believe, sir," said an amazed Merriman.

"It shouldn't be, James. You know from our experiences that we have spies and agents in France and other places and we do know that the French have the same, so why not here?"

"Of course you are right, sir, but it occurs to me that the spy may even be aboard that ship as we speak and if the cargo is intended for Napoleon's army, then from the Netherlands the spy could quickly get to Paris. I will have the captain brought back here, sir, but I am not sure that it would be for the Netherlands. The ship's course seemed to be more north-easterly towards the Baltic."

"It is possible, I suppose, but why would an English ship be taking American arms to the Baltic? We are not yet at war with any of those countries. The Netherlands I could believe, James, after all is said and done the French are there. Another point, that ship sailed from Portsmouth, your Lieutenant Shrigley recognised her, so perhaps they may have picked up the spy there?"

Just then, they heard a lookout's hail from above and a moment later the marine guard knocked on the door to announce, "Midshipman Edwards, sir."

Edwards entered. "Mr Andrew's compliments, sir. Sail, sir, fine on the starboard quarter but he can't see what it is yet."

Merriman leapt to his feet. "Thank you, Mr Edwards. I'll come up."

Chapter Eleven

Engagement with French frigate

Up on deck, Merriman found several of his officers on the quarterdeck with telescopes, trying to identify the newcomer. "Where is, Mr Shrigley?" he asked.

"Masthead, sir," replied Lieutenant Andrews, pointing aloft to where Shrigley was about as high as he could go and using his telescope.

Glancing down, he saw Merriman and descended rapidly. "I can't be sure, sir, but I think it is a frigate though I can see no colours."

"Thank you, Mr Shrigley. Mr Andrews, full action stations, if you please. I want all record times broken. Load the guns with roundshot but don't run them out yet."

Andrews bawled the orders and instantly there was the sound of running feet and the bangs and thumps of the partitions and chests being taken below. Every man had his own place to be and there was frenzied activity as the powder boys ran up to the gundeck with their cartridges of powder and the gun crews started preparing every gun.

Mr Grahame appeared on deck. "What is it, Captain, why action stations?"

"We have seen another ship astern, sir, so I am taking the usual precautions as she has not yet shown her colours. I must ask you to go below if it is a Frenchman."

Mr Grahame was a non-combatant and, in view of his position as an important representative of the Treasury and indeed the Government, he had to be kept as safe as possible.

Merriman walked up and down for a few moments, frowning at his thoughts, everybody else keeping out of his way as far as possible. Another hail came from the masthead lookout, "Deck there, she's definitely a frigate, sir, but she's not flying any colours yet."

That was suspicious in itself, as a British ship would not be afraid of flying her colours but a Frenchman may not, hoping to take them by surprise. Merriman made up his mind.

"Mr Andrews, lower another boat and bring us closer to our captive so that I can hail her." He seized a megaphone and shouted, "Mr Merryweather, I'm sending another boat over. I want all the prisoners and your people back here. Leave the brig without sail on and let her drift. We can collect her later." He turned back to the officers standing beside him. "Now then, gentlemen, once we have everyone back aboard I'll have the prisoners taken and fastened below. Then, Mr Andrews, have our boats secured astern and we'll turn to face this new ship."

That was soon done and, within the same time, the other frigate was hull up on the horizon. "I'm sure she's French, sir," said Shrigley, "judging by the cut of her sails and her sheer."

"I agree with you, Alfred. We will have to fight her."

Just then another hail came from aloft, "Another sail, sir, coming astern of the frigate. I can only see her topmasts but she looks to be a bigger ship, sir."

"That settles it, gentlemen. I'll fight a frigate but if the other ship is a French seventy four we cannot fight the two of them together. If we can see that it is one of the Channel Fleet chasing the frigate, then so much the better and then we will engage."

The *Lord Stevenage* had now turned and, on the larboard tack, was bearing down onto the French frigate which was on the starboard tack. If neither of them gave way they would meet head on.

Merriman had already determined that the other ship was French and he could attack her before the third ship came up to them. The frigate confirmed his decision by opening her ports and running out her guns. Every one of his crew was waiting expectantly to see what Merriman would do. He looked round at the excited faces and then beckoned to First Lieutenant Andrews and the Master.

"Gentlemen, this is what I intend. All the guns should be loaded with roundshot. We will pass on her larboard side. With this strong wind her heel will prevent her guns opening fire on our masts and rigging which is the usual French ploy."

He studied the other ship for a few moments more then said, "If their crew is as bad as it was on that French ship we towed into Portsmouth, then they may not handle their ship as well as we can. Therefore I will try and trick them. Mr Andrews, you will remember how we dealt with the corvette *Sirene* in Bantry Bay in Ireland, I'm sure. Well, I'll try the same now. I want the ship handled like lightning so issue the orders and we'll have the courses off her as well."

Andrews grinned. "Aye-aye, sir. No reason the trick won't work again."

The courses, the big lower sails on each mast were furled before a fight to try and avoid the risk of fire.

"Mr Henderson, I want you and your mates to watch for my signals. We will turn to larboard first and then, if he turns to meet us, we will steer hard to starboard and then to larboard again to bring us level with her. But be ready for a change of orders. It all depends on what the Frogs do. Do you understand?"

"Yes, Sir, I understand. Have no fear, the lads are up to it."

The series of shouted orders by Andrews ceased and Merriman saw the men ready on the sheets and braces. "Mr Bristow, as soon as your guns bear, open fire, starting with the for'ard guns, don't wait until all bear at once."

Lieutenant Bristow was commanding the larboard battery and he too grinned up at Merriman. "Aye-aye, sir."

Merriman thought, *I'm committed now, I just hope the Frenchman doesn't try the same trick*. He watched keenly to see the first sign of the French ship changing course, then he could wait no longer.

"Now," he roared.

The men on the big wheel hauled it round and the stern immediately started to swing as the rudder moved over whilst the seamen were hauling on sheets and braces to swing the sails round. At once the French ship started to turn, slowly, the captain could be seen shouting and wildly waving his arms but all was confusion on her deck as seamen ran to their places to handle the sails at their unexpected orders.

"Now," roared Merriman.

The *Lord Stevenage* changed course again and swung the other way with her bowsprit seeming to miss the frigate's fore rigging by inches as, with her men hauling madly on the sheets and braces, the *Lord Stevenage* began to turn again to pass alongside the larboard side of the frigate as the helm was put over again. Her two big bowchaser guns on the fo'c'sle fired as one with one ball smashing into the figurehead and the other hitting the foredeck rail and smashing the foremast pinrail of the frigate. The 'Smashers' on the fo'c'sle joined in and the shells landed on the French ship's fo'c'sle and burst, spreading death and carnage among the Frenchmen gathered there.

On the gundeck, Lieutenant Bristow could be seen running from stem to stern controlling the firing of the guns, ensuring that no excited gun captain fired before the gun crews could see their target. The guns crashed out, one after another, with the balls smashing into the French ship at gundeck level, most of them creating havoc as guns were upended on to screaming men and timbers between the guns smashed sending sprays of lethal splinters to kill or wound others.

But as the *Lord Stevenage* passed by the French ship, the guns toward the stern, which had not been struck by Merriman's cannon shot, began to reply. It was a bit raggedy, to be sure, but nevertheless hitting Merriman's gun crews as they hastened to reload, causing death in their turn. On both ships, marksmen in the mast tops were shooting down on the other ship's decks.

Merriman saw one of his two new midshipmen, a white-faced, terrified, Evans, struck down by a musket ball which hit his shoulder and threw him backwards. A body fell from above and crashed onto the netting spread above the deck to catch falling objects. It was one of the marines with his throat torn open by a musket ball and his lifeblood pouring out of his mouth, spreading out on the deck below him as if his heart, not knowing the man was dead, still pumped two or three times. Two marines on the quarterdeck were hit simultaneously as they fired over the hammock nettings. They collapsed, lifeless. One of the men on the wheel was slumped against the rail, coughing up gouts of blood before he too slid sideways and was dead. Another man had already replaced him, such was the discipline of the British Navy.

Merriman ran to the rail to look down on the gundeck." Mr Bristow, we are turning to pass her stern. I want every gun of the larboard battery that can, firing into her."

"Aye-aye, sir. Mr Bristow's wounded and taken below, sir," shouted Lieutenant Shrigley. "I am in command down here now, sir." He turned, shouting orders to those gun crews who had managed to reload.

On deck, Merriman shouted orders to bring his ship round the French ship's stern - which bore the name *Carmagnole* - and his guns spoke one by one as they found a target, punching through the stern windows and killing or wounding scores of men on the gundeck.

He became aware of a seaman standing breathless beside him. "The other ship, sir. She's a seventy four and one of ours, the old *Conqueror* I think, sir. I shouted from aloft, sir, but with all the noise you didn't hear me."

"Good, thank you, back to your post. Mr Andrews, bring her round and we'll pass her stern again and give our starboard battery something to do. Mr Shrigley, have the starboard guns ready for their turn."

As the *Lord Stevenage* turned, they saw the Frenchman's mizzenmast begin to lean over. Then it fell, crashing over the larboard side with men entangled in the ropes like flies in a spider's web, most of them destined to a horrible death by drowning. Then somebody managed to drape a white sheet over the stern and it was all over.

Merriman shouted, "Mr Andrews, take a party of well-armed men and marines over to accept their surrender. My compliments to the captain with my apologies, I cannot go myself. Secure the powder room and, oh, you know what to do. This ship will stay astern of the frigate ready to fire another broadside into her stern if need be."

The fighting was over but there could be no rest for Merriman. Various people were waiting to report and doubtless he would have to go to report to the captain of the other British ship, who was certainly senior to himself to be in command of a bigger ship. He looked ruefully down at his blood-splashed trousers and his old seagoing coat. Taking a deep breath, Merriman looked at the men waiting. "Mr McBride, how many?"

The ship's surgeon looked up, absently wiping his hands on his blood-soaked apron. "Six dead, sir," he said gesturing to the bodies laid out on the deck, "and twenty wounded, some seriously others not so."

"Thank you, Mr McBride," said Merriman, turning to the carpenter and the bos'n. "And what have you to tell me? Mr Brockle, you first."

"Nothing serious, sir. Some of the rigging will have to be replaced but my men are working on it now. The sailmaker will have a lot to do though."

"Thank you. Mr Green, what have you to report?"

"The ship is sound below, sir, no water in the well. There are two gun carriages to be replaced. I can repair one but the other is past it. Some timbers and rails are smashed but nothing that we can't put right, sir."

"Very well, thank you, so now you had better get started," replied Merriman.

A cough behind him from Midshipman Green caught his attention. "Signal, sir, the other ship, sir, signals 'Captain to come aboard when convenient'. They are sending a boat with some officers in it, sir."

That was considerate of him, thought Merriman, looking over the side to see two lieutenants ready to climb aboard.

"Permission to come aboard, sir," called one and on Merriman's reply in agreement they were quickly on board and meeting Merriman on his quarterdeck. The senior man touched his hat. "Lieutenants Curtis and Bartholomew, sir. Captain McMasters sent us over to see what help you might need."

"Thank you, there are no repairs we cannot do ourselves, but..." Merriman stopped as a thought struck him. "There is that brig you can see over there. We had captured her before that frigate showed up. She is full of muskets and such, intended for France. I left her to drift and brought all the crew aboard here, they are confined below, but if you could ask Captain

McMasters, with my compliments, if he could bring that ship back and provide a prize crew, I would be vastly obliged. I will visit our wounded and talk with Mr McBride the surgeon, then go over to see your captain as soon as I can find a fresh uniform."

Down on the orlop deck it was like a scene from hell with wounded men swathed in blood-soaked bandages leaning up against the timber of the hull but saying little. Others were moaning, screaming and sobbing. The deck was covered in blood and swabs and Merriman snarled at one of the loblolly boys to clean it up. McBride was leaning over a man on the crude operating table who was writhing and screaming, "Messmates, 'elp me, don't let 'im cut off me leg, please."

But a strip of leather to bite on was thrust between his teeth and McBride's assistants clung grimly on to the man, who Merriman could see was one of the bos'n's mates. McBride was quick. In a few moments the knife and saw removed the man's leg which was thrown into a tub containing other limbs and parts of limbs. By then the man had stopped struggling. McBride bent over him and opened an eye. He shook his head and straightened up.

Noticing Merriman standing there, he said, "I hope you're satisfied, Captain. Six dead up on deck and two more here, including this poor devil. Some of these others will be permanently damaged and will have to be sent back home, though what kind of a life they have to look forward to, God only knows. The rest of them will recover and be useful again in time."

Merriman looked sadly round at the men. He knew that he was to blame for their agony. If he hadn't attacked the frigate, these men would be alive and well, but it was duty, duty to which every man was bound.

"Thank you, Doctor" he said. "I know you have done your best. Make sure that those that can, have an extra tot of rum, I know it will help a little."

As he turned to climb the companion way, a voice called, "Lads, Cap'n's come to see us, cheer up. I 'eard him promise us an extra tot."

Merriman peered at the man in the gloom of the smoky lamps.

"It's me, sir, Biggins, an' I still 'ate them Frogs, an' I'll soon be at 'em again, you'll see." He fell back with a grimace of pain.

Merriman touched his hand and said, "I know you will, Biggins. I want to see you jumping about the deck waving a cutlass again soon."

The man had a hatred of the French and was a bit simple, probably due to the severe wound to his head received years before. He was fond of practical jokes but the men tolerated him and even thought of him as a sort of mascot and kept him out of trouble.

Merriman turned to the Doctor and asked, "How is Mr Bristow?"

"In his cabin, sir. Hurt badly but he'll live."

Merriman returned to his cabin feeling less sure of himself in the face of the grit and courage shown by those men, who had no choice but to do whatever he ordered, even to die.

And so, the big seventy four went after the brig, put some men aboard and they both came back and hove to. By then Merriman's cabin was nearly ready and Peters, his servant, had brought everything up from below and sorted out and brushed his best uniform. In no time his boat was ready and Merriman seated himself in the stern and was rowed over to meet Captain McMasters. He took Grahame with him as his documents would inform Captain McMasters what their mission was.

He was welcomed aboard by the usual ceremony and met by the captain himself with his officers with him. "By the gods, Captain, it is a pleasure to meet you, sir, and your companion. Come below and tell me all about yourselves and why you are here."

Once seated in McMasters' great cabin, so much bigger than his frigate's cabin, Merriman began to introduce himself but the Captain held up his hand to stop him and bellowed, "Bricks." A man appeared and began to dispense drinks. The captain explained, "I call him 'Bricks' because he was a bricklayer and I can't get my tongue round his Welsh name. Now then, gentlemen, to business. I know who you are, Captain Merriman, from the Navy List but your friend…?"

Merriman hastily introduced Grahame who explained who he was and showed the captain his orders from the Government. Then he said, "Captain Merriman is under my orders to take me where I have to go, sir. I must go urgently to Copenhagen to see the Ambassador there, but I can say no more."

"Very well, gentlemen, it sounds important so I won't question you further on that subject, Mr Grahame." He turned to Merriman, "Are you the Captain Merriman who was involved with the abortive French invasion of Ireland a few years ago? Captured an important French spy, I believe."

"I am, sir, and Mr Grahame was with me then. However I must report to you, sir, my recent actions. We saw that small brig acting strangely, almost guiltily, so I stopped him. His hold is full of American guns, bayonets, and powder and shot, probably intended for the French in the Netherlands. My lieutenant found a letter, sir, written in French giving details about our ship movements in Portsmouth and also the Admiralty's plan to assemble a fleet for the Baltic, so I think one of the crew must be a spy or certainly there must be a spy in the dockyard and possibly even in the Admiralty."

He paused for a moment and then continued, "Normally I would appoint a prize crew and send it back to Portsmouth, but I am already men short, eight dead and others badly wounded, and I must continue with our orders without delay. As for the frigate, sir, whilst I was dealing with the brig she appeared on the horizon heading directly for us so I took the crew of the brig, eight men and the captain, aboard my ship, sir, and confined them below. I left the brig to drift knowing I could recover it later."

"I watched your action with the frigate, sir, every move you made, and I cannot say that I have seen a finer ship to ship action. I must congratulate you. I have been chasing that damned ship for nearly two days, in fact I thought I had lost her in the night. She slipped out from Dunkirk, our blockade is spread too thinly you see, but she was spotted and I followed. What about this brig you captured? I put a prize crew aboard as you requested. Do you want them to take her back to Portsmouth?"

"That would be best, sir, if you are agreeable, and the same must apply to the frigate. I cannot spare the men or the time to do it."

"How badly is she damaged, Captain, she lost a mast of course but is she fit for the journey back to Portsmouth?" asked McMasters.

"I can't say, sir, my Lieutenant had not reported back to me when I left to come here, but apart from the mast there must be a lot of damage to her gundeck and a lot of dead and wounded men there."

"Very well, Captain. I can arrange all that and I will escort them both back home. If you will give me your written report before we part, including what you know about the French spies, I will ensure that you will get all due credit for your actions. This affair will yield us both a nice bag of prize money, though of course that for the brig will be entirely yours, but we will share that for the frigate."

"Thank you, sir. There is one other thing, I have the brig's crew under guard on my ship, so if you are agreeable, sir, I propose to press them to make up my losses. If one of them is a spy, we shall find him."

Captain McMasters agreed and so, with thanks for the hospitality, Grahame and Merriman departed, Merriman promising that his report together with the spy's letter would be sent over as soon as possible.

Back aboard the *Lord Stevenage,* Merriman found his first lieutenant ready to report about the condition of the frigate.

"Not too bad, sir, the mizzen mast is the worst but there is chaos on the gun deck. Bodies everywhere and several guns and carriages smashed. The captain is dead, sir, and I left a lieutenant in charge of sorting it out with the rest of the men, albeit under the careful watch of our men."

"Thank you, David."

Merriman turned and looked at the damage to the *Lord Stevenage*, a lot of it already repaired. The ship looked almost ready to face another battle. Men were still scrubbing blood off the deck and cutting off splinters from the deck planks. Some others were aloft reeving some new running rigging.

"I will have to deal with that," Merriman said, pointing to the pile of corpses already sewn up in canvas, "and I'll have to do the same over there on the frigate."

Shaking off his depression, he shouted for his clerk Tomkins to come and copy his reports.

Chapter Twelve

Through the Skagerrak and Kattegat

Four days later the *Lord Stevenage* was approaching the north-western corner of Denmark to turn north-east into the Skagerrak. This led to the Kattegat which, with its many islands, led in turn to a narrow strait and to Copenhagen. Merriman was walking up and down on the weather side of the quarterdeck, sniffing the air and feeling at peace with life although he was careful not to show it in case the officer of the watch approached him to chat. That was unlikely as all his officers knew that his morning exercise was not to be interrupted. Before leaving the *Conqueror*, he had carried out the necessary service on his own ship for burial at sea, then repeated the same aboard the captured frigate assisted by the senior French officer left alive.

He reflected on the events of the last few days. The *Conqueror*, the big seventy four, had left with the captured prizes and carrying his reports for the Admiralty. They had also taken the brig's captain with them for interrogation. Merriman thought with smug satisfaction that he was now many hundreds of guineas richer. He wondered if the prize money from the two frigates captured off India had reached his account yet, the Honourable East India Company had purchased them promising that their office in London would pay for them. Well, that was out of his hands now.

There was something else that he had good reason to be satisfied with. The eight pressed men from the brig had all proved to be good seamen. Although they had settled down to their places on the Watchbill, probably realising that they were better off there than being sent back to Portsmouth and possible execution, two of them were sullen. They kept to themselves and were slow to follow orders but they were competent enough. He had spoken to them, promising fair treatment so long as they obeyed orders and worked with a will. Of course one of them might be the spy but, short of beating them to near death, there was no way to find out which. He hoped that one of them might accidentally let slip that fact. He had instructed his officers to separate the two of them into separate watches.

Most of the wounded men were recovering well and even young Midshipman Evans was proudly walking around with his arm in a sling. Lieutenant Bristow was still giving McBride cause for concern but when Merriman spoke to him in his small cabin he was quite cheerful. "Be about again in a few days, sir," he said.

Merriman decided that, before the ship reached the Kattegat, he would have some officers to dinner that evening. He called over the midshipman of the watch - young Mr Edwards - and told him, "My compliments to all officers and inform them that they are all invited to dinner this evening, except the duty watch, of course. That will include the master, the doctor and Mr Grahame and one of you midshipmen too, and then send the cook to me."

"Aye-aye, sir," said the delighted Edwards, dashing off, doubtless hoping he would be the one selected.

The word spread rapidly and smiles appeared on officers' faces. The apprehensive cook came running up to the quarterdeck and Merriman told him to prepare a good meal and to use another one of the pigs. "Be sure to produce plenty of crackling, remember," Merriman said.

Retiring to his cabin, he told Peters and Tomkins what they would have to do that evening and then he sat to consider what Mr Grahame and he would have to do in Denmark. The marine sentry knocked and called, "Mr Grahame, sir."

Grahame entered with a smile on his face and said, "Thank you for the invitation, James. I am told that we might expect roast pork."

"Yes, sir. I thought it about time I had everyone together again, sir."

"Look here, James, we have known each other for several years now and I would be pleased if you would use my given name which as you know is Laurence. Now I would like to talk about what we are to do over the next few days and weeks."

"Yes, sir, sorry, I mean Laurence. It will take me a while to get used to that. I too have been thinking about the reception we might receive when we sail into Danish waters and Copenhagen. Will we be fired upon, do you think?"

"I certainly hope not, James. As far as we know we are not at war. We shall have to proceed as we discussed and hope for the best."

Dinner that evening was an enjoyable affair. All were present except the watch, even Mr Bristow arrived on shaky legs, determined not to miss anything. The cook did not disappoint them. The pork was done to a turn and the crispy crackling served up in manageable pieces. Peters and Tomkins served the food and then began to serve wine.

"I hope you will like this wine, gentlemen," Merriman said. "I bought it in Portsmouth and it has been in the bilges ever since. It was recommended to me by Admiral Fitzherbert himself. I apologise for the shortage of fresh vegetables, I hope we can restock in Copenhagen but meanwhile we have apple sauce and potatoes to go with the meat. Now, before we set about the food, I would like you to remember what Samuel Pepys said, 'Strange to see how a good dinner reconciles everybody'."

They fed well with plenty of jesting and bonhomie but Merriman sensed that there was an undercurrent to the gathering.

After they had eaten and cheese and wine had been served, Merriman looked at the company. Lieutenant Bristow was looking pale faced and tired although he had made a valiant effort to eat. He was obviously ready for his cot. Evans, the midshipman, was nearly asleep with a contented grin on his face.

Merriman rapped on the table and said, "Mr Evans, I would be obliged if you would wake up and propose the toast as is your duty."

The bleary-eyed youngster struggled to his feet, grabbed his glass and squeaked, "Gentlemen, The King," before collapsing back onto his chair.

Grahame said with a smile, "'When the wine is in the wit is out', an old proverb I think and I think also that our young friend has eaten and drunk enough for two of them. Indeed, as

Shakespeare says in Much Ado About Nothing, 'He is a very valiant trencherman'."

There was much laughter and Merriman called for his servant, Peters. "Take Mr Evans below to his berth, Peters, we won't get much sense out of him now."

The conversation continued until Merriman said, "I believe this has been a pleasant evening and I am sorry to bring it to a close but tomorrow morning we will be approaching Danish waters and I want all of you alert for what might happen. So then, goodnight, gentlemen."

The officers dispersed with many thanks to their host, two of them helping Bristow to his small cabin.

Chapter Thirteen

Delayed by gales

Dawn came, a cold wet dawn with dark clouds overhead and a biting north easterly wind. No other ships were visible and so the men were dismissed from the usual action stations. The ship was heeling over to larboard and Merriman, bundled up in his heaviest coat, scarf and oilskins and with his hat firmly fixed on his head, was standing on deck holding onto the weather rail. He hoped this weather would not turn into a full gale although it seemed likely.

He frowned and scowled about him. That frown and scowl made everyone on deck keep away from him which was good as he wanted more time to himself to decide what to do if a full gale did blow up to delay the arrival at Copenhagen. Not that he could do much about it if it did other than to run before it or lie hove to under minimal sail. The best heavy weather canvas had been bent on for the last two days and lifelines would be fastened on as soon as necessary. Everything was already secured with extra lashings and the heavy guns especially well secured.

However the weather did get worse and Merriman was forced to order the courses furled and the topgallant sails furled as well. A hard and difficult job it was with the topmen battered by incessant rain with showers of icy sleet. With frozen fingers they fought to control the hard canvas and tie the gaskets. Many a seaman had lost a fingernail in the process over the years. With their feet on the footropes they leaned perilously out over the yard to claw the wet and madly fighting sails up to the yards then tied them there. On deck, the men handling the various ropes, buntlines, clewlines, sheets and others were sometimes waist deep in water as, with the ship pitching and rolling, the water came over the foc's'l and weather side by the ton. Spray flew high as the ship hit the next wave full on, sending more water over the foc's'l and pouring out of the scuppers as she rose again.

It was sufficient to make progress under furled topsails, staysails and driver, although making good towards their destination was painfully slow, indeed in the worst of the gale the ship hove to was fast losing the ground she had made over the last two days. Despite his scowl, Merriman was enjoying himself. This was real sailing and no mistake. He had full confidence in his ship and crew to weather the worst gale that blew up.

He thought back to the gales and typhoon winds he had experienced in the past in both the Indian Ocean and the Caribbean. His thoughts were interrupted by an apologetic Peters, "Sir, Mr Grahame is asking for you, sir," he whispered as confidentially as he could above the noise of wind and wave. "The gentleman is ill again, sir."

"Very well, Peters, I'll come below."

The officer of the watch was Lieutenant Merryweather, very capable of handling the ship with the master and Midshipman Small, so satisfied they were attending to all required, Merriman went down to see what Mr Grahame wanted.

Poor Grahame had suffered greatly from seasickness in the past but had apparently got over it. Now it took really erratic movements of the ship to affect him. In his cabin Merriman found the wretched man crouched over a bucket bringing up the remains of his breakfast. He recovered slightly and with a ghastly pallor on his face, collapsed back into his cot while Peters removed the bucket and left a clean one in its place.

"Ah, James, thank you for coming. I can hardly move and I thought I was cured of this damned Mal-de-Mer. Anyway, how is this weather affecting our voyage to Copenhagen?"

"Well, sir, I'm sorry, Laurence, we are making slow progress. I must emphasise the 'slow' as the wind is blowing from where we need to go and constant tacking is needed. But we will get there in time just maybe a day or two later than I had hoped."

"I know you are doing your best, James, and you can't control the weath…" Grahame groaned and climbed out of his cot to make use of the clean bucket.

Merriman left, indicating to Peters that his services were needed again.

The bad weather continued for another three days before abating and allowing the ship to proceed easier in the right direction. As *Lord Stevenage* entered the huge bay, the Skagerrak, between Norway and Denmark, the weather eased still more and they made better progress. On deck, Merriman asked First Lieutenant Andrews and the Master Mr Henderson to join him in his cabin.

"I think it is time we had extra lookouts aloft, David. We have Norway to larboard and Denmark to starboard and they can be considered to be one country. And of course there is Sweden also. We will be well out of range until we enter Kattegat where the narrowest part is the strait between the extreme north eastern tip of the island of Zealand and the Norwegian coast, which is some two and a half miles wide. There are forts on either side and we might expect to be fired upon if we are at war with them although if we keep to the centre we should be safe enough. Mr Henderson, have you been here before and how are your charts?"

"Yes, sir, I've been here twice before and the charts are as up to date as they can be although there are no really reliable charts available from the hydrographic office of the waters close inshore at Copenhagen."

"Good and thank you. I know that many of the officers have been studying those charts most keenly so have them keep on studying them. Further south the strait widens out before we come to Copenhagen where it closes to only just over two miles wide. There will be forts on either side and more to defend Copenhagen. There are sandbanks too, so I expect you to watch the depth, Mr Henderson, using the leadline if you need it."

"Aye-aye, Sir", replied the master. If he was annoyed that the captain thought he had to tell him his job he was careful not to show it.

In the event, no batteries fired from either shore and the ship passed near to the big Trekroner fortress at the entrance to the harbour of Copenhagen. The fort's name meant Three Crowns, symbolising the crowns of Denmark, Norway and Sweden, and it was armed with huge cannon frowning down over the harbour entrance and supported by other forts and batteries. As the ship neared the outer harbour, a boat under sail approached and a little man shouted officiously, "I am the harbourmaster. Who are you and what do you want?" His English was so bad that Merriman could only just make out what the man was saying.

"We are bringing a diplomat to visit our embassy here and we need fresh water and vegetables," shouted Merriman. "And a pig or two," he added as an afterthought.

"Very well," replied the man after some thought. "Follow me and anchor where I tell you. We'll send water and supplies out to you." As they complied the man shouted again, "Nobody must leave your ship until our inspectors have spoken with you."

As they anchored with the expected cannon fire of salutes ringing out, Merriman was looking round with interest, realising that they had anchored within cannonshot of a Danish warship. *Not taking any chances it would seem,* he thought.

The next visitor was a man dressed in some sort of uniform. He stepped aboard and raised his hat politely to Merriman. "I am the customs officer, sir, and I must see your documents," he said in good English.

Merriman took him below to where Mr Grahame was dressed in his best outfit and waiting to show the man his diplomatic credentials. "I am here to visit the British Embassy as a representative of King George and his Government, sir. I hope there will be no delay," said Grahame.

"No, sir, all is in order and you may go ashore as soon as you wish," said the customs man, turning to Merriman. "Captain, I am told by the harbourmaster that you need fresh water so I will arrange for a water hoy to come out to you and somebody will sell you fresh vegetables. However I must insist that nobody is to go ashore except for Mr Grahame. For you, sir, I will arrange for a small carriage to take you to your Embassy."

Eventually a small carriage appeared and Grahame was rowed to the dockside where he found the customs officer waiting to ensure that none of the boat's crew slipped ashore. While that was happening, a sort of barge was being rowed out by men using big, heavy sweeps. It came alongside *Lord Stevenage*. It was the water hoy and Merriman was requested to send his empty barrels over to be filled. Another customs man was on board with two very obvious soldiers suspiciously watching to ensure that that was all that happened.

Another small boat came alongside with vegetables and a trussed pig. After Merriman paid what was owed, the boats returned to their places in the harbour and Merriman called his officers to his cabin.

"Gentlemen," he said, "Mr Grahame will be gone for only two days and whilst he is gone we must try and record all the activity in the harbour and make drawings of what we can see of the harbour defences. But we must not be seen to be taking a lot of interest in that. Only one or two of you at a time must study what you can with a glass and others of you can sit out of sight and write it all down. Bearings of forts and anything that will be of interest to our fleet if we have to attack. Mr Small, here is some paper, I know you to be good at drawing and you must take your turn with the glass and then try and draw what you see."

Small nodded and took the paper.

"Captain St James, it is many weeks since we last had our usual sword practice and I am feeling a bit rusty, so I think we should continue with it as often as we can. You can show me some more tricks."

"Aye-aye, sir," responded the smiling marine. "I do have one or two more tricks up my sleeve, and remember, sir, the saying, 'No skill in swordsmanship however Just, can secure against a madman's thrust'".

Ever since they had met aboard Merriman's sloop *Aphrodite* some six or seven years ago, St James, an accomplished swordsman, had been teaching Merriman some of the finer points of swordplay. He' also include some tricks which he had said were not in the usual fencing instructor's book of rules and were regarded as not suitable for gentlemen to use.

"That is all very well if you are fighting a duel, sir, with seconds and a referee," St James had said. "But the purpose of this exercise is to get your blade into your opponent before he gets his into you, so rules be damned."

Chapter Fourteen

Merriman makes notes of the defences

Two days of careful but casual observation yielded much that was new. Most of the Danish ships that were no longer fit for sea service were being moored along in front of the city. They were still heavily armed and formed a line of floating batteries terminating at the northern end at the huge Trekroner fort. North of the fort were moored two ships-of-the-line and other floating batteries. Batteries could also be seen along the coast behind the ships and any attack would have to be made along the channel between the floating batteries and a large shoal named the Middle Ground which restricted access.

By the time Grahame returned, Merriman was pleased with what they had learned and charts with all the defences clearly marked with their bearings from *Lord Stevenage's* anchorage were finished. Although they dared not use boats for checking soundings, Merriman had made careful note of where the main channels seemed to be by watching the movement of larger vessels at each stage of the tide.

There had only been one incident which cropped up. In his cabin early one morning, Merriman was disturbed by shouting on deck and came up to see what was happening. At his appearance, Lieutenant Merriweather turned to face him and reported, "One man overboard, sir. He jumped and is swimming to that American ship over there. I shouted for him to stop and come back but he is still going. He must be trying to desert."

Merriman seized a megaphone and shouted, "You in the water, this is your captain speaking. I order you to come back or you will be shot."

For answer the man turned on his side and made the common two-fingered gesture before swimming further.

Merriman gestured to the two marines standing next to him and simply said, "Shoot him."

Marines were normally posted on deck with loaded muskets, there to prevent deserters from jumping ship and the two of them instantly fired at the man in the water. One ball struck the water by his head but the other hit him in the back. He twisted round and, with his two fingers raised, he disappeared. The only sign of his passing was a rapidly dispersing stain of blood.

Merriman turned from the rail and was returning by the side deck to the quarterdeck. He had barely reached there before he was thrown violently down by a seaman screaming, "Bloody murderer! You bastard, he was my brother. I'll kill you, I will." The man attempted to stab Merriman in the back with his knife.

Merriman managed to turn soon enough to grasp the man's wrist and divert the blow before a marine clubbed the man with the butt of his musket and he fell senseless to the deck.

"Are you all right, sir?" asked a worried Lieutenant Andrews, helping him to his feet.

"A bit shaken, David, but otherwise intact, thank you," replied Merriman looking down at the unconscious body by his feet. "Have Mr McBride look to the fellow and then put him in chains below in the punishment cell. I'll see him later."

"Aye-aye, sir," said Andrews calling for the Master-at-arms to deal with him. "You were lucky that time, sir. If that marine hadn't been so quick to hit him you could have had his knife between your ribs."

"I know, Mr Andrews. Now which marine was it?"

"Jones, sir, he's here."

Merriman turned to see a red-faced and grinning marine behind him. "Well done, Jones. You saved my life, thank you. Captain St James, I want this man to have a commendation in his record and if you think him ready he might be promoted to corporal, I've noticed him before for his actions in the West Indies."

"Aye-aye, sir, I'll see to it," replied the Marine Captain. "Come with me, Jones." He led the grinning marine below.

Eventually Grahame returned to the ship in a gloomy mood. "Nothing to report, James," he said. "At the embassy I spoke with many people but nobody could say for certain if this treaty, the League of Armed Neutrality, had actually taken place. One diplomat, Mr Vansittart, with his ears in the right places, did say that he believed it had been signed under pressure from the Tsar and he did tell me that the Danes had rejected the British ultimatum. And, he said that a French warship had passed here into the Baltic, maybe to visit the Russians but he couldn't be certain why. I think you should make sail and take the ship out of here as quickly as you can, we might be fired on at any time."

In the event they were not fired upon except once when they were nearly out of the Kattegat when an odd battery on the Norwegian side with an over optimistic gunner did fire. Fortunately, they were well out of range and watched the ball skipping along the surface of the sea in a series of hops before it disappeared. As they turned the tip of the island of Zealand and into the Skagerrak, Merriman breathed a big sigh of relief and smiled at Grahame. "Where do we go now, sir?"

Grahame said, "I'm not sure, James. I would like to go to Oslo to see one of our people there but the way in is very narrow and if the Norwegians are definitely against us we wouldn't reach the city. I think Bergen might be our best choice. It is a big trading port and England has many friends there. I believe even some English people live there, but even so I can't say what our welcome would be like. Anyway I think we should try it. I'll think it over some more."

Although it was now well into September, they were fortunate that the weather was still fair but as the ship turned north along the coast of Norway there was a definite chill in the air. As they approached Bergen, keeping well out at sea, Grahame made up his mind.

"I'll go ashore, James, by boat and as close to the town as possible. You know, we have done this many times before. You lie well out of sight of land and come back in at night to look for my signal lamp. If I'm not there on the second night you should assume the worst and leave to report back to the Admiralty and Lord Stevenage."

"Take care, Laurence. We don't know but that every man's hand will be against you."

"James, don't worry so. Remember I am an old hand at this and beside, 'I have the cloak of night to cover me from their sight'. That is from Romeo and Juliet, I think."

"Indeed it is, but please remember another old saying, 'a fair day in winter is the mother of a storm'. The weather is fair at the moment but if a storm does come up I will have to stay well out at sea and not be able to pick you up for more than two days. Discretion must be the better part of valour for you, as some proverb says."

Merriman and Grahame had the habit of trying to outdo the other in quoting proverbs and quotations from Shakespeare and other authors.

Grahame smiled. "I think you have the better of me there, James. Are we near enough so you can put me ashore tonight?"

"Yes, but where exactly do you want to be put ashore, north or south of Bergen?"

"North would be best, James, more of the town and merchant's warehouses and homes are there on the north side of the harbour and I should have no difficulty in getting into where I need to go. If there is bad weather or I am suspected, I may have to move along the coast to the north of the town to be picked up."

And so, under reduced sail and with a gentle breeze, the *Lord Stevenage* ghosted inshore and quietly anchored, with lookouts all round the ship. Grahame was rowed to the shore in the gig with Midshipman Small at the tiller. When they reached land, a burly seaman carried Grahame ashore to keep his boots dry.

When the boat was recovered, Merriman asked Mr Small if all was well. "Oh yes, sir. Mr Grahame said he thought he knew exactly where he was and sent us back here."

The ship quietly made for the open sea and at dawn she was in the middle of a wide expanse of water with no other ship visible. Merriman kept the crew busy with all the normal routine while cruising peacefully and slowly up and down to keep as near as possible to where Grahame had landed. He and St James were on deck practicing swordplay with interested officers watching, but the peace was not to last.

At three o'clock of the afternoon watch a lookout hailed. "Deck, there," he shouted, pointing north. "Two ships astern, sir. One may be a frigate."

Merriman made up his mind in an instant. He ordered the ship to change course to starboard and increase sail to keep as far away from the newcomers as he could. Meanwhile he sent a keen-eyed seaman aloft with a telescope.

A few minutes later the man was back down on deck reporting, "It's a frigate, sir. Seems to be escortin' a fat merchantman, mebbe goin' to Bergen, sir. If they keep on course they'll pass astern of us, sir."

"Back aloft with you. Keep me informed of any change."

"Aye-aye, sir," the man replied then disappeared up the shrouds.

Merriman pondered, have they been seen and if they had, what would the frigate do? He could do only one of two things, continue to Bergen or turn after them and chase. He thought that if the frigate came to find out who they were, they would lose it in the coming dark, but it was possible that the alarm would be given and other ships might come out tomorrow. Anyway, for now they had to go inshore again to look for Grahame's signal lamp.

There was no signal that night and by morning the weather had deteriorated so much that the *Lord Stevenage* was forced further out to sea and couldn't get back to the point where Grahame's lamp could be seen. Two days of freezing weather and a gale which seemed determined to drive them further offshore ensued. It was only on the fourth night that Merriman dared to bring his ship close inshore. Desperately worried that Grahame had been captured or even shot, Merriman cruised slowly northwards from Bergen as Grahame had suggested. It was only in the early hours before dawn that the signal was seen and Grahame brought back. He had to be almost carried on board.

The poor man was in a wretched condition, weak and bedraggled, wet and shivering with cold. He nevertheless managed to tell them that the alarm had been raised and ships were looking for them. Instantly Merriman ordered a change of course straight out to sea to get as far away from the coast as the ship could before dawn. McBride, the ship's doctor, was ready and had Grahame stripped of his wet clothes and wrapped in several blankets in his cot in no time.

Dawn's pale light showed no sign of other ships and a very relieved Merriman had the doctor summoned to his cabin. "How is your patient, Doctor, will he be all right?"

"I believe he will be, sir, given time to recover. He is still asleep and I would like to keep him like that until he wakens normally. He isn't a young man, sir, but fairly fit and strong so he should be all right."

It was almost mid-day before the doctor climbed on deck and announced to Merriman that Grahame was awake and needed to see him.

"Can he be moved, Mr McBride? If so, can you bring him to my cabin and then tell Peters to bring hot coffee and something for him to eat."

The doctor disappeared below and, after checking that all was well and scanning the horizon again, Merriman left the deck and returned to his cabin. There he found Grahame, still wrapped in blankets, drinking hot coffee and nibbling on a piece of bread. He still looked so bad that Merriman was moved to say, "'Meagre were his looks, sharp misery had worn him to the bones.' From Romeo and Juliet, Laurence."

Grahame raised a feeble smile. "By the gods, James, I had nearly given up hope when your boat suddenly appeared and the men practically dragged me aboard. I really think that I am too old for all this excitement." He took another sip of the hot coffee then continued, "Do you think I could have something hot to eat? I'm starving."

"Of course," said Merriman, turning to the sound of footsteps. "I think this is Peters bringing it now."

Peters it was. He bustled in with a tray bearing fried pork, fried potatoes and other vegetables and laid it in front of the hungry man. Grahame fell to with a will and Merriman said no more until Grahame sat back with a contented grunt.

"Now then, James, I must tell you what happened to me in Bergen. I found the town and the house of a friend easily enough.

I knocked on his door but the man who opened it was not my friend, he was a Norwegian and in uniform as well. When I couldn't answer in Norwegian he became suspicious so I ran and they have been hunting me for three days. I haven't learned anything but that they are suspicious of strangers. When the weather turned bad I knew it would stop you coming to collect me so I didn't dare stay on the coast until last night when you found me. It was a complete waste of time, James. I learned nothing of importance and now I think we should head back to England to report to our masters."

As they crossed the North Sea and headed for Chatham on the Medway, the nearest naval port and dockyard to London, Merriman told Grahame of the incident of the deserter and the attempt on his own life. "So you see, Laurence, I think these men were the spies from Portsmouth, brothers, and Irish to boot. One of them was shot trying to escape and the other is confined below after being laid senseless by a marine. Mr McBride tells me that he is now fit enough to be questioned. So, with your approval, I will have him brought up here."

The order was passed by the marine sentry and a few minutes later the small form of an anxious midshipman, announced by the same sentry, came in. "Mr Bristow's compliments, sir, he thought the man not fit to bring to your cabin. He's filthy and smells, sir, so he is being sluiced down on deck."

"Very well, Mr Evans, thank you. My compliments to Mr Bristow and ask him not to bring him down until he is cleaner and dry."

"Aye-aye, sir," said Evans and he bolted from the cabin.

"He has been in the punishment cell in chains and his only companion a bucket for his needs so I'm not surprised he is in a filthy state," smiled Merriman grimly. "And he has been living on bread and water though the men wanted to give him nothing at all."

The thump of the sentry's musket butt on the deck announced the arrival of Lieutenant Andrews, Lieutenant Bristow, the Master-at-arms, and two big marines holding the prisoner between them. The man was still dirty and of course unshaven but, as Andrews said, "Better than what he was, sir, and he doesn't stink as much. I gave him an old shirt and trousers from the slop chest, sir. His own filthy ones have been thrown overboard."

Merriman and Grahame looked the man up and down. He was bare footed and, although he tried to look indifferent and stare at his feet, it was clear that much of his spirit and antagonism had gone.

Merriman began, "What is your real name? Not the one you gave us when we took you prisoner."

The man didn't answer, still looking down on the deck, so Merriman continued, "I shall read out the charges against you and then we will hear what you have to say in your own defence." He held up a piece of paper with the charges listed. "First, that you acted as a spy in England and tried to pass information to the French. That is treason for which the penalty is hanging. Second, that you and your brother did attempt to desert, another hanging offence. And third, you struck a superior officer and tried to kill him which is also a hanging offence. What do you have to say?"

The man tried to draw himself erect, spat on the floor and almost snarled, "I'm Irish, I am, an' proud to be so, though me Mam were French. Me name is Patrick Casey an' me brother was Sean before you murdered him, you English bastard. Yes we spied on the navy in Portsmouth but another man in London gave us money and sent that letter for us to deliver an' I don't know 'is name. And it weren't treason. I were fightin' for my own country, Ireland, God bless 'er".

Merriman didn't react to the abuse and said, "Your brother knew the penalty for desertion, didn't he? A severe flogging at least, or death if I am minded to take that action. As for the attack on me, there is only the one penalty specified in the Admiralty Articles of War – death. Have you anything else to say before I pass sentence?"

"Bloody English, thieves an' murderers, think you own Ireland, don't you? Well there are a lot more like me, not afraid to fight for our country. So a curse on you, sitting there in yer fancy uniform. I 'ates the lot of ye and I'm not afraid to die."

Merriman told the Master-at-arms and the marines to take the man out but keep him handy which brought on another tirade of cursing until one of the marines clamped a big hand over the man's mouth and they dragged him out.

"Now then, gentlemen, what do you think?" Merriman asked each of the two officers and Mr Grahame in turn.

All were agreed; the man should be hanged. "He's a bad lot, Captain," said Grahame, and Bristow said, "For what he did to you, sir, he should be hanged, never mind the rest."

"Very well then, Mr Bristow, please ask the marines to bring him in again."

The man was now white-faced and trembling as at last he realised what awaited him. He wrenched himself away from the marines and flung himself down on his knees babbling about mercy for sinners until the marines dragged him to his feet. Merriman was not a cruel man, but he really had no choice. As Captain of the ship he was duty bound to follow the Admiralty Articles of War.

He hardened his heart and said the required words, "Seaman Casey, you have been found guilty on all counts and you will be hanged immediately. Take him away."

The man was led out. Merriman sat quietly for a long moment before speaking again. "A nasty business, gentlemen. Mr Andrews, please be kind enough to tell the master-at-arms to make the arrangements and the bos'n to prepare a noose. Then have the whole crew mustered to witness punishment."

It didn't take long. Merriman was on the quarterdeck with all his officers and marines. All the men gathered in their various watch stations for'ard, waiting to see what would happen. Merriman read out aloud the appropriate part of the Articles and then nodded to the marine guard. They dragged Casey to where a noose hung from the mainyard with men waiting on the tail of the rope to haul him up. The wretched man screamed before the rope tightened round his neck and he was hauled up. His bladder loosened and he twisted and kicked for three or four moments before he hung still.

There was silence for a few seconds before an unknown voice called out, "He deserved it for what he did to you, sir. What do you say, lads, a cheer for the Captain?"

His answer was a loud roar of approval from the men before they were dismissed. Merriman was surprised to hear Bristow say, "They all wanted a hand on the rope, sir. We had to select them. It seems that that the men think a lot about you, sir."

"Yes, I think they do," grunted Merriman before retreating below where he called Peters to bring him a glass of brandy.

Chapter Fifteen

Merriman meets Admiral Nelson

Merriman stared gloomily out of the carriage window. It was pouring with rain and the city was dank, dark and miserable. The streets were littered with sodden, indescribable rubbish and the smell ... well! He tried to breathe no more than absolutely necessary through the kerchief he held to his nose. Mr Grahame was with him and they were making their way to a hotel Grahame knew of.

He had brought his ship creeping into the Medway River, carefully avoiding the changeable mud banks on either side, to Chatham dockyard. Merriman and Grahame had decided to take the ship there and then a post-chaise to London as that route would be quicker than sailing round to Portsmouth and then coaching back to London.

They had not sent word ahead of their arrival in London but, once they were settled into the hotel and wearing fresh clothes, a messenger was sent to the Admiralty. They were trusting that Admiral Sir David Edwards would be eager to hear what they had discovered during their foray to Denmark. Indeed, they were swiftly summoned.

The usual harassed lieutenant took their names and showed them into the waiting room. Surprisingly, the room was almost empty, apart from a single lieutenant worriedly biting his lip and a midshipman, little more than a nervous boy, who almost cringed when Merriman, a captain, looked at him.

The inner door opened and another captain emerged, smiling broadly. He walked past, hardly noticing anybody there. *He's had some good news,* thought Merriman. *Maybe a new command.*

The lieutenant and the midshipman were called next, to come back after some twenty minutes with the lieutenant white-faced and the boy in tears. Obviously they had received bad news or a censure, perhaps the end of their career in the Navy.

Merriman recalled the time he had been waiting here when a pasty-faced and miserable captain had emerged from the inner sanctum with his career in ruins. He had been the captain of a frigate which suffered a mutiny, only put down with difficulty by the loyal men. That frigate was renamed the *Lord Stevenage* and given to Merriman when he was promoted to Post Captain. He was brought out of his reverie that one man's misfortune had delivered good news for him by the lieutenant calling, "Sir David will see you now, gentlemen."

The big room was just as Merriman remembered it with its ornate, coved and plastered ceiling, the weather repeater on the wall so that the wind direction could be seen at a glance. A beautiful, highly polished mahogany table was in the centre of the room. Admiral Edwards sat at it with another officer near him. Merriman was startled to realise that this man must be the famous Admiral Horatio Nelson. The pinned up sleeve of his coat confirmed it.

"Ah, Merriman," said Admiral Edwards. "Maybe you know my other visitor, eh?"

"Yes, sir, I do. It is an honour to meet you, my lord, your name is known everywhere," said Merriman, bowing.

"Oh never mind that, Captain. Admiral Edwards has been telling me about your exploits round Ireland and the Caribbean Sea. I hear that you were in India defeating pirates when I was trouncing Napoleon's fleet at Aboukir Bay in Egypt." Nelson sat for a moment staring at Merriman. "Merriman? Merriman? I remember a very good frigate captain, Joseph Merriman, from when I was a lieutenant. Are you related by any chance?"

"Y-y-yes, sir," stammered Merriman. "He was my father, but he is dead now, sir."

"Ah well, it catches up with us all in the end. You have my condolences."

Edwards spoke, "Sit down, gentlemen. Mr Grahame, my lord, is the Treasury's agent and reports to the Prime Minister and Lord Stevenage. He was with Captain Merriman in those events you mentioned and is just back from Copenhagen."

Nelson nodded to Grahame and turning to Merriman, asked, "What have you found out in the Baltic about defences and such, and are those countries really allied in that damned treaty?"

"Yes, sir, I believe they are but Mr Grahame can tell you more about the diplomatic side of that. I have my report here, sir, and charts of the defences of Copenhagen harbour. They are as complete as we could make them from looking round from where the ship was forced to anchor. The Danes wouldn't let any of us ashore, sir, except for Mr Grahame."

"Well done, Captain," exclaimed Nelson, almost leaping up from his chair, his one good eye alight with interest. "Spread them out on the table and let me see."

Merriman had brought with him copies of the charts which had been laboriously copied by his clerk Tomkins and he unrolled them as requested and stood back.

"My word, Captain Merriman, these are wonderful. I see you have made estimates of the depth of water there also."

"Yes, sir, I couldn't use a boat with a leadline without the Danes noticing but I took note of the sizes of different ships and where they passed at all states of the tide."

"Excellent, Captain," said Nelson and, turning to Admiral Edwards, he said, "I definitely need this officer under my command in the events to come. As always I will be desperately short of frigates and I would be happy to have Captain Merriman with me in the Baltic if that could be arranged."

"Very well, my lord, that can be arranged. Now, Mr Grahame, tell us what you know about this damned treaty."

Grahame duly obliged and, whist he was recounting what he knew, Merriman was nearly hugging himself with delight. He was going to join the famous Lord Nelson. What action and excitement awaited him? Nelson was not as big as he had imagined, a slight, erect figure, well known in the Navy for his deeds and injuries. His lost arm was clearly signified by his empty sleeve but Merriman was surprised to see that his eye injury did not show, there was no disfigurement and the eyeball was visible but cloudy. Nelson was noted for his impetuosity in battle and frequent disobedience of orders but equally well known as a great naval tactician with many victories to his credit.

Merriman was aroused from his thoughts by Admiral Edwards speaking to him. "So that is settled, Captain. You will join the fleet presently assembling at Spithead before moving to Great Yarmouth. Admiral Nelson is to be the second in command under Admiral Sir Hyde Parker and you will be part of that fleet, attached to his Lordship here. Where is your ship now?"

"Chatham, Sir David. We judged it would be quicker if we came here by post-chaise from there."

The Admiral nodded. "Yes probably, Captain. I'll have your orders drafted immediately so don't leave without them. Now I must speak to Mr Grahame alone so if you would wait in the next room."

Merriman was only waiting for a few minutes before Grahame appeared again. "I'm afraid it's bad news, James. Lord Stevenage is very ill and as I am the senior agent of the Treasury, I am charged with replacing him temporarily, so I shan't be with you this time."

Merriman was aghast. Lord Stevenage was his patron and responsible to a large degree for Merriman's advancement.

"Ill? How ill is he, can we visit him?"

"I don't know any more, James. He is at his country estate and not able to carry out his duties at present, indeed if ever again. I shall be going to see him immediately so, if you wish to write a letter, I will be pleased to take it to him. But you have your orders so you will not have time to visit him."

March 1801, the fleet sails for the Baltic

In October of the year 1800, Merriman brought his ship round to Spithead to join the fleet being assembled for the Baltic. And there the ship stayed, swinging on her mooring. The only excitement was when another Ship-of-the-Line arrived to join them, bringing the total up to twelve plus several frigates, brigs and bomb-ships.

During that time, Merriman was at his wits' end to find new exercises for his crew to keep them sharp and up to his required standard. The men were getting bored with inactivity and fights had broken out, one with knives but thankfully the others were just fisticuffs although Merriman censured the men and only punished the two knifemen.

On a happier note, some captain decided to arrange boat races between all the ships, each boat crew to consist of no more than eight men and a midshipman on the tiller. There were so many ships wanting to compete that they were divided into three groups with the winner in each group to compete in the final.

Naturally this caused much excitement, and careful selection of the strongest oarsmen from each crew with much good natured banter between the men such as, "Don't know why you was picked, Jacko. You 'ave trouble pullin' a belayin' pin, ne'mind an oar," and, "Don't forget that you all 'ave to face the same way when rowin'," and, "Bernie, you dozy bugger, don't fall asleep will yer?" The officers were as keen as the men and small wagers were made between them. Two days had been allowed for selection and practice until the day of the race dawned and the boats assembled in their groups.

Of course the smaller ships, sloops, brigs and bombships with smaller crews to pick from formed a competition among themselves and the bigger Ships-of-the-Line and frigates made up the other competition. The winner of the smaller ships came from the brig-sloop *HMS Harpy,* eagerly urged on from another boat by their captain, William Birchall. Then came the turn of the boats from the bigger ships. The boat from the *Lord Stevenage* won in the first heat by a good margin and rested as they watched the two other groups.

Then it was the final, with a boat from the seventy-four gun *HMS Monarch*, a boat from the thirty-six gun *HMS Blanche* and the boat from Merriman's ship, *Lord Stevenage*. At a trumpet blast from the Flagship, all three crews set off, pulling madly. At first the other two forged ahead, but Midshipman Greene carefully kept his crew at a slower stroke until he could see that the other boats were slowing, their crews having almost exhausted themselves. Then he urged his men on to a supreme effort and passed first one and almost passed the other, only losing the race by half a boat's length. Other boats from the ships followed with men shouting to and cheering for their mates.

As the weary men climbed back on board, Merriman met them and shook hands with them all. The purser, Grummage, was also there with a tray of tin mugs and a bottle of rum from which he grudgingly provided the boat's crew with a double tot.

"That was well done, men, very well done," said Merriman. "You beat all the boats from the bigger ships and nearly beat the lot of them."

"Yes, sir," said Greene. "We did and if the course had been fifty yards longer we would have won."

That excitement lasted for days with spirited discussions going on all round the ship and Merriman was pleased to see how much morale had improved. As he toured the ship on his weekly inspection he was met by grinning men in each watch and at his duty station.

After that nothing happened until January of the next year when it was confirmed that Admiral Sir Hyde Parker was to be in command with Rear Admiral Nelson to be second in command. Again there was a delay until the end of February when the fleet received orders to get underway for Great Yarmouth. That short voyage gave the crews of all ships the opportunity to be practiced in heavy weather sailing.

Admiral Sir Hyde Parker, at the age of sixty-one, had just married a young eighteen-year-old girl and he took her to Yarmouth with him to stay at an inn in the town. Of course this news gave the seamen the opportunity to come up with all kinds of ribaldry as the news rapidly spread from ship to ship.

Merriman was on the quarterdeck, staring at the shore, when he heard one of the marines say to his fellow, "Admiral Parker! Rambunctious old goat, he is. No wonder he wants to stay ashore." That was one of the least offensive comments and Merriman had difficulty in keeping his face straight and pretending not to have heard. "Didn't think he had it in 'im, mate," said another. "No, but I bet he had it in somewhere," laughed another.

Merriman coughed to remind them that he was there. Just then the mail boat came alongside with a bag of letters and orders. There was one from the Admiralty Prize Office confirming that the money from the sale of two frigates captured in India had been paid into his account and another letter from Helen reporting on events at home and repeatedly using phrases of endearment he would not have wanted anybody else to see.

Eventually, Admiral Nelson, recently promoted to Vice Admiral of the Blue, arrived at Yarmouth on the eighth of March. He expressed his annoyance that the Commander-in-Chief was still ashore with his wife, planning a ball for the following week. Nelson called all the captains to a meeting aboard his Flagship, the *St George,* to discuss the situation in the Baltic and what they may find it to be. Nelson was angry. "We should sail immediately, gentlemen. Every day we lose means that Denmark can increase its defences and, if the ice in the Baltic melts enough, we could have the Russian fleet against us as well. We can't sail until Admiral Hyde Parker joins us but I think our friend is a little nervous about dark nights and ice, or perhaps he prefers a warm bed," he said mischievously.

There was some laughter and Nelson continued, "Gentlemen, I don't believe you all know Captain Merriman here. He was in Copenhagen some months ago and he has made excellent notes of the defences there and some of the soundings. Copies of his own chart with all the main features of the defences are being prepared for each of you as fast as possible. I suggest you study Captain Merriman's own chart here and feel free to ask any questions."

They all wanted to see the chart and soon the questions came thick and fast. Merriman could hardly answer one before another. Nelson said, "You will all notice that the bearings of each fort and the floating battery are taken from the one point where his ship, the *Lord Stevenage,* was forced to anchor. Now, gentlemen, make your own notes for now and your copies of the chart will be sent out to you."

It transpired that Nelson had written a letter to the Admiralty about the delay and the effect of that was that Hyde Parker received formal orders to set sail immediately. So, on March the twelfth, the fleet set sail for the Baltic. It was a strong force of fifteen ships-of-the-line, two fifty gunships, and frigates, brigs and bomb ships.

Chapter Sixteen

The battle of Copenhagen

Merriman, in common with most men in the fleet, was excited to see the coast of Norway to larboard and Denmark to starboard. The fleet eventually reached the narrows between the Danish shore and the batteries on the Norwegian side leading into the Kattegat, but there was no cannon fire from either side and the fleet sailed on heading for the much narrower strait between Kronborg Castle in Denmark and the shores of Sweden. They kept well away from the Danish side and fortunately the Swedish guns remained silent.

There was great speculation amongst the officers on the quarterdeck and Lieutenant Bristow summoned up the courage to ask Merriman if he knew the Admiral's plans.

"No, Mr Bristow, I don't, but it wouldn't surprise me if the fleet was divided into two squadrons, one under Admiral Hyde Parker and the other under Admiral Nelson's command. Splitting up to be able to attack from north and south behind that big shoal called The Middle Ground would make sense to me. But we can only wait and see."

They had not long to wait. There was a great flurry of signals from both Flagships and the fleet began to separate as Merriman had foretold. The Commander-in-Chief gave Nelson ten ships-of-the-line, all with the shallowest draught and all the smallest ships in the fleet, including some of the frigates, bombships and fireships, while he would stay with the rest of the fleet to the north-east, ready to engage the northern defences.

Nelson moved his flag from the *St George* to the *Elephant* which had a shallower draught, and then both squadrons anchored to the north of Copenhagen while Parker, Nelson and other senior officers went aboard two frigates for a reconnaissance. One was the *Amazon* and the other the *Lord Stevenage*. Merriman was surprised to hear the signals

Midshipman Small call out, "Signal from Flag, sir. 'Prepare to receive senior officers', sir."

Merriman hastened below to change into his best uniform after telling his officers to do the same and to order the side party to close up. He was back on the quarterdeck in time to hear somebody say, "It's the Admiral, sir, both of them actually."

Admiral Hyde Parker was the first to come aboard, closely followed by Nelson and a retinue of Army officers and some naval captains to the squeal of bos'n's pipes and the rigid lines of marines at the present arms.

"It's good to see you again, Captain Merriman," said Nelson. "Admiral Parker, sir, this is the captain who drew up the latest charts showing the Danish defences."

"Well done, Captain," said Parker. "I'm sure they are right but I want to see for myself as does Nelson here."

"Can I interest you gentlemen in a drink? I have some exceedingly fine claret below," said Merriman, trying to be the perfect host.

"No time for that, Captain, we need to see all we can before it's too dark to see," replied the Admiral. "Set sail at once."

They approached Copenhagen from the north, as close as possible while staying just out of range of the biggest guns in the batteries. Merriman had a leadsman in the fore-chains taking soundings as fast as he could while Lieutenant Bristow noted them all down. Then the two frigates moved south-eastward past The Middle Ground to see the defences there.

"Just as you said, Captain. Your description of it all was excellent," Nelson told Merriman, "and I congratulate you on a task well done. Now I would like to try your claret while we sail back to the fleet."

In Merriman's stern cabin, which must have seemed small to the Admirals after their spacious cabins aboard the flagships, he apologised for the lack of space.

Nelson interrupted him. "Captain Merriman, don't worry. We have all been frigate captains in our turn and know what it is like. Some of my happiest memories are of when I was a frigate captain." He took a sip of the claret served by a nervous

Peters and continued, "By Jove, Captain, this is a fine claret. Do you not agree, gentlemen?"

There were sounds of agreement from the rest of the group and Peters hastily topped up the glasses.

When the visitors had gone back to their own ships and *Lord Stevenage* was safely anchored, Merriman all but collapsed in his chair, looking around his cabin with relief. All captains want their ship to appear at its best with so many senior officers aboard and he had been worried that something would go wrong. But Nelson had taken him by the arm as he was leaving and said, "You have a fine ship, Captain. I've seen many but none better than yours, sir."

At last Nelson's squadron was under way and, in the last of the daylight, passed down the outer channel and anchored to the south of the Middle Ground. That night, under cover of darkness, Captain Foley of the *Elephant* - now Nelson's Flagship - spent hours being rowed up and down the channel between the Middle Ground and the Danish line of ships, now named the King's Channel. He had his men take soundings and returned to report that the channel was suitable for an attack. He also confirmed most of Merriman's estimates.

At dawn on board the *Elephant* the signal halliards were busy with instructions to the ships-of-the-line to weigh anchor and proceed into the channel in the pre-determined order with *Agamemnon* in the van. However she ran aground before entering the channel as did both *Russell* and *Bellona*. This necessitated a change of strategy and the next ship took the lead. Nelson's plan called for all his ships to sail in line ahead with the first one anchoring by the stern near the first Danish ship. Then each ship was to pass the one ahead and anchor in turn abreast of a Danish ship only about two hundred yards away. As soon as the first ship reached its allotted place at about eleven thirty, firing broke out and, with only a gentle breeze, the gun smoke hardly cleared, becoming denser as each pair of ships in turn opened fire.

To the south of the fleet, and in the screen of frigates and smaller ships, Merriman knew that the fleet was attacking

Copenhagen. He paced up and down the quarterdeck, not an easy task because of the number of sailors and marines there at their posts and all the activity as the guns were loaded. Trying to retain his demeanour as the imperturbable captain, he was nonetheless desperate to see what was going on.

Finally he yielded to the desperation to know more and slowly climbed up the mizzen shrouds with his own glass. It was hopeless, great clouds of smoke clearing only slowly from the southern end of the line meant that he could only see the first two British ships and their opponents, as well of course as the three grounded ships, which were engaging the southerly Danish batteries, though at extreme range.

Merriman had been in many ship to ship actions and he knew what damage, death and destruction would be happening between the two lines of warships at what was point-blank range. There would be men half-blinded by gun smoke and deafened by the noise of the cannon. Between decks it would be a scene of horror as men were cut down by cannon balls or lethal splinters of wood. The dead would be dragged to the centre of the deck and the wounded sent down to the orlop to the tender mercies of the ship's surgeons. On the various upper decks, the officers would be the targets of opposing sharpshooters and wouldn't dare stand still for a moment. The many huddled corpses would show the success of the enemy marksmen.

On Merriman's ship, his officers shared his frustration as they vainly tried to see what was happening while the gun crews peered out of the gun ports. Certainly the frigate captains had been told to stand off, but they had also been told to help where they could. However, it was no part of a frigate's duties to tangle with a bigger enemy and one would be blown to splinters under the broadside of a big two or three deck ship.

Suddenly Merriman saw an opportunity and called First Lieutenant Andrews to him. "David, you can see those grounded ships trying to get their boats away to take reinforcements across to the big ships. It is a long row for them and I think we can help. If we go alongside one of them, though not too close because of the shoals, we can take men off her to add to the reinforcements. We will anchor by the stern while our boats are filled and then we can tow them all to the line of our ships. Give the orders, Mr Andrews." Merriman switched back to a formal tone, glad they now had something to do.

The plan worked, the *Lord Stevenage* approached the nearest of the grounded ships, the *Agamemnon*, and dropped a stern anchor. That involved heavy work for some of the crew to get the heavy cable through the ship. Merriman hailed her captain, Robert Fancourt, and explained his plan. Fancourt was the senior officer but he readily agreed and Merriman's boats were soon being loaded from the *Agamemnon* and ready to be towed. Merriman ordered the stern anchor cable buoyed and cut and the ship slowly gathered way with her own boats behind. They collected *Agamemnon's* boats as well, with Merriman in the first boat.

Closer to the line of battle, the damage to the ships became more apparent. The worst damage seemed to be on the Danish ships, several masts were down on the first ship with all the yards lying across the decks and streams of blood running down the side. There the guns had ceased and British marines could be seen on her deck. Merriman ordered a boatload of men to be cast off to go to the aid of the British ship, then they passed slowly along the line to the next British ship. This was still firing at its opponent and they cast off another two boats. An officer on the quarterdeck waved his hat in acknowledgement and then they reached the next ship, the *Elephant*, Nelson's flagship, which was heavily engaged with another Danish ship.

Of course they were seen in spite of all the gun smoke and a hail came, "What ship?"

Andrews yelled back, "British, you damned fool. *Lord Stevenage*. Got some men for you if you need them."

An officer appeared at the ship's rail and shouted, "Thank you, send them over. We do need them. Is that Captain Merriman there?" When the assent was given, the officer continued, "Sir, the Admiral thought he saw you and asks that you join him."

Merriman detached another two boats full of men and moved on with the remaining four boats to deliver the men to the next two British ships. Then, having managed to anchor *Lord*

Stevenage, he had himself rowed back to the flagship, feeling more than a little apprehensive.

He climbed aboard to be met by a severely depleted side party then he was escorted by a midshipman to the quarterdeck where Nelson was pacing up and down. He stared at Merriman for a moment and then said, "Disobeyed my orders, didn't you? I'll speak to you later, stay here."

The wind was too light to sail back to their starting position, so Merriman had ordered Lieutenant Andrews to have an anchor dropped. The *Lord Stevenage* slowly swung round and stopped near to, but screened from, the enemy by a British warship. By then, according to Nelson's plan, the bombships were moving down outside the British line to be able to lob their shells over the British ships and on to the Danish ships behind. Once the destruction of the Danish ships at the south end of the line had been completed, they would be able to approach within range of the city, hopefully forcing negotiations with the enemy.

At the height of the engagement, Admiral Parker with the reserve was unable to see clearly because of the smoke and, thinking that Nelson's squadron had been forced to a standstill, ordered his flag captain to have a signal hoisted, a signal to recall all ships. When this message was reported to him, Nelson ordered that the signal should not be repeated. He raised his telescope to his blind eye and said to the flag captain, "I really don't see any signal, Foley. What about you, Merriman?"

Merriman dutifully replied, "What signal, my lord? I can't see one."

Nelson nodded and turned back to the battle.

By now the British had gained the upper hand and at least a dozen of the southernmost Danish ships had fallen silent owing to damage. Gradually the fighting proceeded northwards until all the Danish ships fell silent. The battle was over, apart from dealing with the many corpses of the dead and the hundreds of wounded, both English and Danish.

Nelson, standing apart from all the people striving to report about the state of the ship to Foley, the flag captain, beckoned the still waiting Merriman to him. Eyeing him sternly, Nelson said, "Captain, as I said before, you disobeyed my orders to form a screen to the south. Why?"

"Sir, the orders also said that if we saw a way to help, we should do so, so I did, sir. And there were plenty of other ships in the screen."

Nelson stared at him for a moment then he smiled. "By God, Mr Merriman, you remind me of me at your age, when I commanded a frigate. That was well done," and he punched Merriman playfully on the arm. "Now, as soon as there is enough wind, I want you to proceed southward again. Take two sloops with you and see if you can find the Russians and the French ship which passed by here some days ago. Wait until my clerks can draft your orders and orders for the sloops before you go."

Chapter Seventeen

Merriman reports Russian fleet in Kronstadt

Two days later, Merriman's small squadron had all sail set and were making their best speed to find the Russian fleet or the French ship, although the sloops had to reduce sail a little to allow the frigate to keep up. At dawn, with the ships at action stations as usual, there was no sign of any other ships. The crew stood down for breakfast although extra lookouts were sent aloft. Fortunately the wind had increased to a stiff north-easterly and the three ships were making good time.

Merriman walked over to speak with the ship's master, Tom Henderson. "How long do you calculate it will be before we are near Tallinn, Mr Henderson."

"Mebbe two more days, sir, less if this wind holds, though the sloops could do it in less if they were sent ahead."

Merriman thought about it for a moment then said, "Right, Mr Henderson, we will heave to. See to it please while we signal to the sloops to do the same and for their captains to come aboard."

Lieutenant Upton, the captain of the *Zephyr*, and Lieutenant MacKinley of the *Otter* were both eager young men and urged their boat's crew, racing to see who would be aboard *Lord Stevenage* first. Upton's boat crew won by only a few minutes and Merriman welcomed both of them aboard.

"I'm glad to meet you, gentlemen. Now come below and I'll tell you what I want you to do."

Seated in the Great Cabin, and each with a glass of wine in hand, the two officers listened keenly to Merriman's orders.

"With this wind and your fore and aft rig both of you can sail faster into the wind than my ship can, although she can show a good turn of speed. So I want you to sail far ahead, you Mr Upton towards Tallinn and you Mr MacKinley to go as far as you can to Kronstadt. I am hoping the Russian ships there will still be icebound, but you must keep out of the ice yourselves. When you have seen enough, report back to me. I shall keep sailing on this course as far as possible so you should have no trouble finding me. Is that clear, gentlemen?"

It was not long before both sloops, heeling far over in the wind, were only specks on the horizon, leaving Merriman in a fever of impatience waiting for them to return. Knowing it would be at least another day before he saw them again, he settled down in his cabin to read some Shakespeare, but he couldn't concentrate on the words. His mind kept on wandering to thoughts of home, his wife and little boy, Robert William Edward. That thought made him wonder if he had left his wife bearing another baby, they had certainly been trying hard enough. He smiled at his thoughts.

After eating his solitary meal, he went on deck for his usual last look round, checking the compass and sniffing the weather. Having full confidence in his officers and men to keep the usual shipboard duties done, and to keep him informed of any change in the weather or sighting of any other ship, he turned in.

It was ten o'clock in the forenoon watch before there was a hail from the lookout in the fore-top. "Deck, there," he said, pointing ahead to starboard. "A sail, sir, a sloop, the *Zephyr* I think."

It was indeed the *Zephyr*, closing rapidly under full sail until she rounded to in the lee of the frigate and her captain, Upton, was hastily rowed across to report.

"Captain Merriman, sir, on your orders I got as close as possible the harbour at Tallinn. The ships there are still iced in and there was no sign of preparations for sea, sir, no yards crossed and as far as I could see, with not many men aboard."

"Well done, Lieutenant, but I see that your ship has suffered some damage, what happened?"

"A French seventy-four, sir, that's what happened. I had the *Zephyr* under well-reefed sails so as not to go too quickly to let me see everything I could and, as we rounded the eastern headland, there was the French warship under full sail coming towards us. Naturally I brought the ship round and crowded on all the sail I could. We were faster than the Frenchman, sir, but before we were out of range it fired a bow-chaser and the ball passed through the taffrail, killed two men, holed a sail and splashed into the sea. By then it was nearly dark and so I held that course until I was able to give the Frenchie the slip in the dark before I came looking for you, sir. I hope I did right as I didn't want to give away your position, sir."

"You did, Lieutenant, you did. Now we know for certain that there is at least one French ship of war loose in this part of the Baltic Sea. As soon as the *Otter* comes back, I will send her back to the fleet to report to the Admiral whilst we will try and find it. She was sailing westward when you first saw her, wasn't she? While she was chasing you did she do any more than follow you back past Tallinn?"

"No, sir, she kept right on past there heading west. Of course I am sorry, sir, I couldn't see what she did after I changed course to escape in the dark."

"Don't apologise, Lieutenant. It isn't part of a sloop's job to face up to a frigate, never mind a seventy-four. You would have been smashed to firewood. Remember the old saying, 'Discretion is the better part of valour'. We will turn west and sail under reduced sail in the hope that the *Otter* can find us. If we are to follow the Frenchman I don't want to go further east than I have to. So then, back to your ship and see to the repairs and follow me."

It wasn't until late in the afternoon watch that *Otter* was seen astern, closing rapidly under all the sail she could carry before reducing sail to allow her way to fall off.

"Mr Small, signal to both ships, 'Captain to come aboard', and be quick about it. Mr Merryweather, bring both of them down to my cabin when they are here."

Once all were gathered in his cabin, and Peters bustled round serving wine, Merriman impatiently asked, "Now then, Lieutenant MacKinley, what about the Russian fleet in Kronstadt?"

"All safely bottled up by ice, sir. I couldn't get very close because of the ice but as far as I could judge there seemed to be nothing happening there. Only a few ships had their yards crossed but with that thick ice I don't think they will move for some time. But there is something else, sir, something that I believe to be of some importance. We stopped a small Russian trading ship well out at sea and the captain said that he had heard that the Tsar of Russia was dead. Perhaps if that is true, maybe the Treaty of Armed Neutrality will collapse."

"Well you may be right, Lieutenant. I will write a report for you to take back to the fleet, to Admiral Nelson, together with your own report. *Zephyr* sighted a French seventy-four last night heading west which I will try and find so you must keep a careful watch for it yourself. *Zephyr* was faster and was able to escape and so will you if you keep your eyes peeled. We can't take on a seventy-four so I hope the Admiral will send one or two of ours to deal with it. Wait here until my report is ready. Tomkins, where are you?" Merriman shouted. Almost as if he had appeared out of the woodwork, Tomkins was there. "Tomkins, I want you to add to my report to the Admiral. It is ready I hope?"

"Oh yes, sir, tell me what to add. It won't take me long."

The completed report was given to Lieutenant MacKinley who left at once on his journey back to Copenhagen while Merriman and Upton prepared for their part in finding the French ship.

"Lieutenant, we shall move west by south to see if we can find him. You must stay as close as you can to the shore but avoid any shore batteries and stay within signalling distance of me. Remember, we have captured Copenhagen but he may not know it until he is near to there, unless he finds a fishing boat somewhere which can tell him. So it is unlikely that he will try to get out of the Baltic and will try to retrace his course back to somewhere east or north of us for shelter. You should keep extra lookouts aloft all the time. Now let us begin the search."

Chapter Eighteen

Search for French warship

Three days later, after sailing down the length of the southern coast of the Baltic from the Gulf of Riga and past there to the anchorage and port of Gdynia, nothing had been seen of the French ship. Those two places were the most likely spots to find it because of the suitable depth of water, but Merriman had discounted those expecting the ship to be heading as fast as it could for the exit from the Baltic at Copenhagen.

Lieutenant Upton, with his small sloop, had sailed closer in than could the *Lord Stevenage* but, although there were plenty of small inlets, there was nowhere for a big seventy-four to hide. Once they had reached the island of Bornholm, Merriman decided that he should turn north to explore the hundreds of islands along the coast of Sweden. Of course there were plenty of islands and bays on the east coast of Denmark where the French ship could be hidden but he thought that unlikely as Denmark might now be allied with England.

So he despatched Upton in *Zephyr* back to the fleet to report where he had gone and his reasoning why he was doing so. He hoped that the *Zephyr* might be sent back to find him with the news that reinforcements were on the way, two seventy-fours at least with other frigates and some fast scouting sloops. In the meanwhile he must continue his quest along and among the many islands off the Swedish coast, although he knew it was impossible for his ship to do more than watch the French ship if he found it. He couldn't attack it alone; the *Lord Stevenage* would be pounded to matchwood before he got close and, even if he got close enough to board, there would be far too many men aboard for his own crew to fight. No, finding it and keeping a watch on it was all he could do.

It was a slow and tedious business trying to find a ship among all those islands, made all the more perilous by the possibility of

Swedish warships appearing to find out what an English ship was doing there. Of course, if the Treaty had broken down after the Tsar's death, then Sweden would not want to antagonise Britain on her own, but it must be borne in mind. As the days passed, Merriman became more and more impatient and had his work cut out to try to appear calm and confident. As it was, his frowning face caused everybody aboard to keep away from him if they could.

The further north the ship went the colder it became and sudden fierce icy squalls would spring up out of nowhere meaning more work for the men, first shortening sail to avoid damage aloft and then doing the opposite only minutes later. The Strait of Kalmar between the mainland and the island of Oland was still frozen so they were forced to sail round the island further out to sea. It was a cold, wet, miserable existence. The men were wet through with little chance of drying out between calls aloft and with all hatches battened down the air in the crew's accommodation became more and more foul.

Merriman had spent most of his time on the windward side of the quarterdeck clinging to the shrouds, cold, wet and shivering. Finally he decided that they all deserved a chance of a rest so he determined to find a sheltered place where the ship could anchor and the men have a hot meal.

He called a weary and damp officer of the watch to him. It was the first lieutenant. Trying to be cheerful he said, "I've had enough of this, David. We must find a sheltered place to anchor. I'm going below to see the master and look at his charts. As soon as possible the men must have a hot meal and try to dry their clothing. The hatches can be opened to get rid of the stink."

"Aye-aye, sir. We all need time to recover and dry out. I've noticed how much slower the men are to get aloft. They are worn out but will still do their best for you, sir."

"I know, David, I know. It will encourage them and cheer them up a little if they are told what I intend, so pass the word along. I also remember that though all the chickens were drowned and eaten, I do know I still have the last pig somewhere. As soon as we can I will have the cook deal with it and I shall invite the officers to dinner." Enlarging on his theme he said, "Two dinners, I think, so that the officers on watch the first time can join me on the second evening."

A big grin appeared on Andrews' face. "That would be fine, sir. I'm sure we shall all relish some hot pork, especially the crackling."

However it took another day and a half of fruitless searching for the French ship before they found a good, sheltered anchorage for the *Lord Stevenage* and the men could rest for a while. Of course the Duty Watch had to keep the deck but Merriman ordered that no man should spend more than two hours on watch in the cold. It was surprising how much a hot meal and a rest improved morale aboard. Soon the bos'n and his party were up aloft checking for anything that needed repair while the men below dragged their damp hammocks out to dry in the wind and then opened the hatches to let a blast of cold, fresh air through the ship as they set about the many tasks to do to clean the ship up.

That evening Merriman's great cabin was filled with laughter and the smell of roast pork as the first selection of officers joined him. They were Lieutenants Andrews and Merryweather, Midshipmen Small and Evans, Marine Captain St James and the ship's surgeon Alan McBride. Peters and Tomkins served the meal, not without some difficulty as the motion of the ship was still quite lively. Some of Merriman's fine claret soon had the conversation flowing and Merriman smiled as Andrews said, "Sir, you met Admiral Nelson at the battle of Copenhagen when he came aboard but he was too busy with Admiral Parker to have time for us. What kind of man is he?"

"Well, I met him first at the Admiralty when he was kind enough to congratulate me on our work mapping the defences of Copenhagen. You all know that he is a fine sailor and will keep sail on when many others would reduce it. He is also a good tactician which is why he has won so many battles. As to the man himself, he is friendly and alert and will listen to his officers' suggestions. You all know that he lost his arm, which is made obvious by his empty sleeve, and he is blind in one eye but not disfigured. Indeed you would not know it unless you were quite close to him and could see the eye is bright but cloudy. I believe he is a great Admiral who will win more battles yet."

All of them were listening keenly including Peters and Tomkins, but the two midshipmen were sitting there wide eyed and with mouths agape, doubtless dreaming of being an Admiral.

Alan McBride, the surgeon, said, "I'm sure that all that is right, sir, but he blotted his copybook with his attachment to Lady Hamilton, didn't he?"

There were angry glances directed at the surgeon but Merriman said sternly, "That is enough of that, Doctor. He is a fine officer and his foibles are no concern of ours." To change the subject he turned to the marine officer, "Edward, how are your marines? Cooped up below in all this bad weather you haven't been able to parade them on deck."

"Oh, they are well enough, sir. If needed they will still be able to give a good account of themselves."

The conversation continued long after the plates and remains of the meal had been cleared until Merriman said, "Thank you for your company, gentlemen, it has been a very pleasant evening." That was the signal for all of them to leave, thanking him for his hospitality, all except McBride who Merriman asked to stay.

"Mr McBride, you crossed a line back then. I will tolerate no criticism about a senior officer in public. In private you may say what you like but the Navy. But the men love Nelson and if you had made that remark on deck and the men heard it you might have found yourself swinging from the yardarm. Do you understand?"

McBride nodded shamefacedly. "Yes, sir, I'm sorry, it won't happen again."

The following day the sun appeared and its slight warmth was appreciated by all. By the time darkness fell the ship was as smart as new paint, the 'tween decks well ventilated, the hammocks and the men's clothing dry and everything had been checked for damage. There had been some repairs to do but Merriman declared his satisfaction. The men had had hot meals, only boiled salt meat and biscuits to be sure, but they were well used to that sort of fare. In the evening, the second half of the pig was served in the great cabin to the officers who had not been there the previous time and Merriman was again well pleased with the evening.

Chapter Nineteen

The Plague Ship

Merriman was up on the quarterdeck the next morning as daylight was only just appearing in the east. There was no sun to be seen. The sky was a solid mass of grey cloud and the wind was freshening. He sniffed the air and decided that they were in for another gale. The officer of the watch was Lieutenant Bristow and others were coming onto the quarterdeck, so Merriman ordered that as soon as the men had had their meagre breakfast, he wanted to get underway to continue the search. Men were already busy on the gundeck preparing for action stations, which was the normal exercise aboard a King's Ship first thing at daybreak. Lookouts were aloft as soon as there was enough light for them to see beyond the bay in which the ship was anchored. One shouted down, "Deck, there, nothing, sir, no sail in sight."

An hour later the ship was sailing northward with courses furled and with a strong wind on the starboard quarter. The short break had certainly refreshed the men and Merriman was pleased to see smiles on their faces with the usual badinage between them. *It won't last, they'll be wet and cold again soon enough*, he thought gloomily. The gale he had forecast was soon on them but they were well clear of the coast and so had plenty of sea room.

Fortunately the gale was not as bad as Merriman had expected and by the middle of the day, it had blown itself out. The sun came out in time for the officers to use their sextants to confirm their latitude. Merriman and the master insisted that even the midshipmen practised the art of position finding, although the two new boys had widely differing results. The calculations of young Evans eventually succeeded in placing the ship down in the middle of Denmark. They would learn.

Two more days of searching yielded no sign of the ship they were seeking and so Merriman decided against going any further north. It had not been possible to search every inlet and island and they had probably missed it, so he had the ship turned to head south again to look further, possibly in places they had missed. Three more days passed with the weather improving every day until by the third day they had plenty of sunshine and it became quite warm, more than expected so far north. By the next morning the ship was shrouded in fog.

As Merriman appeared on deck in the early hours of the morning, Officer of the Watch, Lieutenant Shrigley, reported their course and weather details as normal. He added that he had sent more lookouts aloft and on to the fo'c'sle. "Can't see a thing, sir. Could be a fleet out there and we wouldn't see it. Might get better when daylight appears though."

"Quite so, Mr Shrigley, but have the men prepare action stations as usual but quietly, no shouting or drumbeating to warn any enemy who may be out there."

"Aye-aye, sir, no noise. When this damned fog lifts we might see our quarry."

There was only a light breeze and the fog hung on until almost ten o'clock in the forenoon watch when finally it began to thin out. Immediately the foretop lookout shouted, "Deck, there!" He pointed forward to the starboard side. "Masts, sir, three of 'em, but none of topsails look right."

"Mr Shrigley, aloft with you and take your glass. Tell me what you think."

The agile young officer climbed the shrouds like a monkey and as he watched Merriman mused that he himself couldn't do that as fast as he used to. The fog was now rapidly disappearing and it didn't take long for Shrigley to return to the deck.

"It is a seventy-four, sir, by the look of it a French ship but I can't read the name on the stern. As you can now see, sir, the courses are furled somewhat messily and the topsails are not even drawing properly and not braced round. She isn't making much headway. I couldn't see anybody aboard either, sir."

"Most unusual, Alfred, most unusual. I wonder…" Merriman summoned his officers to him and told them what Shrigley had seen.

"Must be something wrong, sir. I would expect to see their gun ports open at least and they must have seen us," said Andrews.

"They could be luring us into a false sense of security," said Marine Lieutenant St James.

"That is possible of course so we shall take no chances," replied Merriman. He thought for only a moment before ordering, "I'll have the courses furled, gentlemen. Mr Henderson, bring us abreast of her, slowly, but out of gunshot and keep us on the windward side of her."

"Aye-aye, sir," replied the Sailing Master, shouting orders to the crew and helmsmen.

"What do you think may be wrong, sir?" asked a daring Midshipman Edwards.

"I don't know, Mr Edwards," replied Merriman. "But I do have an idea. Mr Merryweather, Mr Shrigley, I want you both aloft, as high as you can go and take you telescopes with you. There must be something you can see to explain that ship's condition."

Both officers were quickly aloft and studying the ship keenly as *Lord Stevenage* slowly passed. Suggestions were bandied about between the officers on the quarterdeck and some of the gun crews were hanging out of the gun ports to better see what could be happening.

Incensed by their actions, Merriman bellowed, "This is serious, gentlemen, we are supposed to be at action stations. Have those gun crews at station, not behaving like washerwomen. We don't yet know but that we shall be fired on."

On the quarter deck the chatter died down and the crew sheepishly returned to their places.

Merryweather hastily climbed down and white-faced he reported, "Sir, I think they are all dead. Bodies are lying all over the deck and nothing is moving. Most of them seem to have removed their clothes and seem to have scars on their bodies."

"Have they now? Mr Bristow, my compliments to Mr McBride and would he please come on deck immediately?"

The surgeon soon appeared and Merriman drew him aside out of earshot of the others. "Mr McBride, I have a suspicion that there is fever aboard that ship." He related all that had been seen. "I will turn the ship and we'll pass back alongside her but well away on the windward side. I would like you aloft with a glass to see what you think."

"But, sir, I've never been higher than the side rail, I'm not a topman."

"I know that, Alan, but it is important. I'll send two experienced hands up with you to keep you safe. We don't want to lose our only Doctor do we?"

McBride nodded. "I'll try, sir, but I must confess that I am scared of heights."

So Merriman detailed two good topmen to assist the surgeon and, when well past the big seventy-four, he had his ship turned to pass back alongside it so that McBride could have a good look. Once past, the doctor climbed slowly down with the men holding him and crossed to Merriman.

"Sir, it is as you thought. It's a plague ship, we must keep well away."

"Tell me exactly what you saw, Mr McBride, exactly."

"Well, sir, from up there I could see all that Merryweather reported but I was able to deduce more. The men are mostly dead, just slight movements from a few of them. I think it is either typhus or typhoid, both cause a red rash and or swellings in the groin and armpits. Most of them will have thrown off their clothes to scratch themselves more easily. I've not seen anything like it before."

"Poor devils. What causes it, Alan?"

"Well, as you know, sir, I was unable to finish my medical studies but I have read as many medical books as I could get hold of and it seems that these fevers are caused by drinking contaminated drinking water or eating polluted shellfish. They also spread rapidly in the crowded and cramped conditions below deck where men are breathing the breath of already suffering men. We have no cure for it, sir."

"What would you recommend I should do then?"

"We can't help so I would suggest that the whole ship should be burned, but none of our men should go aboard to do that, and I repeat, none of our men should go near it," replied the doctor.

"Thank you, now I must think about it." Merriman paced up and down the quarterdeck, pulling at his ear and with a scowl on his face. Every man on the quarterdeck kept well out of his way and tried to look busy in case they drew his attention.

At last he stopped his pacing. "Mr Andrews, I believe we can finish with action stations but keep all the lookouts aloft. See to it if you will."

"Aye-aye, sir," replied Andrews, turning away to shout the orders.

Merriman beckoned to one of the midshipmen on deck. "Mr Evans, please go down to the magazine and ask the gunner, Mr Salmon, to come up on deck, I wish to speak with him. And, John, don't run, just walk."

"Aye-aye, sir," stuttered the boy, disappearing below in amazement. The captain knew his name, that lofty figure remembered his name. He must write home about it as soon as he could.

The gunner duly climbed up to the quarterdeck to report to his captain. "Mr Salmon, as I'm sure you already know, that ship is a plague ship and must be burned, but nobody must go near it to set it afire. This is what I propose." Merriman proceeded to discuss various ideas he had before asking, "Mr Salmon, you should know the capabilities of our carronades probably better than I do, what do you think?"

The man thought for a few moments before replying, "I don't think a normal shot will set it alight, sir. A round shot wouldn't and a grape shot wouldn't unless one of the musket balls happened to hit some of the ready use powder, if there was any lying about on deck anyway, sir. But your second idea could do it. If I could have a few minutes to make some calculations, sir, I'm sure it can be done."

"Very well, Mr Salmon, calculate away and then tell me what you will need."

Salmon was back on deck in less than five minutes holding a bar shot in his grubby hands.

"Yes, Mr Salmon, what have you decided?" asked Merriman.

"Well, sir, I think this should be what you want, sir." Salmon held up the bar shot which was simply two half cannon balls joined by a bar and said, "If we tie oily rags round this bar they should ignite when the gun is fired and we could perhaps increase the chance of burning if we could put a bottle of oil in last, also wrapped in oily rags, though the only thing I can suggest is a wine bottle or a rum bottle, sir."

"That seems like the solution, Mr Salmon. Have you calculated the powder charge for that, considering that we want it to land on the deck which is much higher than ours, but not to overshoot and go right over the ship?"

"Oh yes, sir, I calculate that at about three degrees elevation and two thirds of the usual charge it will be about right. We should stand off about three hundred yards, sir."

"Very good then. If you prepare three or four of these firebombs of yours in case one doesn't reach or goes over after which you could alter the charge."

"Yes, sir, have I your permission to use any bottles I can find and ask the bos'n for some of his oil?"

"Of course you can, Mr Salmon, but make sure they are empty bottles. My steward can find some wine bottles for you. See to that, Mr Merryweather, if you will."

The officers had been listening closely to what had been said and Lieutenant Bristow ventured the comment, "Do you think it will work, sir?"

"Yes I do, Mr Bristow. The gunner is very experienced and if his calculations are correct, that will set that ship alight." He pondered for a moment and said, "I want a pump rigged to wet the fo'c'sle before we fire and kept manned ready in case of accidents. And I want the ship kept at three hundred yards to begin with after Mr Salmon fires, until that ship is burning well and then moved off to five hundred yards or more."

He walked to the rail on the starboard side which was facing the French seventy-four before calling Captain St James over to him. "Captain this could be a difficult thing to ask, but I want some of your marines, the best marksmen, on the quarter deck with their muskets loaded. You see, there may be some poor souls still alive on board that ship, but they will be infected and we can do nothing for them, therefore, if any man shows himself I want him shot. His only other choice is to die of the fever or burn to death. Shooting is the kindest thing we can do. Do you agree, Captain?"

"Yes, sir, it would be best. We would do as much for a damaged animal. But the longest range our muskets can fire with any accuracy is less than two hundred yards though one or two of my men can do a bit better. A volley from the rest of the men as well might be best. I'll arrange it at once."

The gunner appeared again, carrying all he would need and he called the carronade crew to him to prepare the carronade for firing. The powder charge was rammed home, then a ring of wadding was rammed in and the bar shot wrapped in its oily rags followed. The last item was a wine bottle wrapped in rags. The gunner carefully checked the elevation of the barrel and the distance between the ships before he turned to Merriman and said, "Ready, sir, but I would like all men to leave the fo'c'sle when I fire."

Once that had been done and Merriman nodded to him, the gunner pulled the cord to the flintlock on top of the gun and it fired. Every man who could watched to see what happened next. The missile burst into flames as it flew through the air but it fell short, striking the gunwale of the French ship and exploding as the bottle of oil shattered.

"A little more powder next time, I think, Mr Salmon, but that was well done, try again."

Within minutes the experienced gun crew had the gun ready. The gunner took hold of the cord again and looked to Merriman who nodded. This time the shot was perfect and it landed on the deck of the French ship. "Deck, there," yelled the lookout on the main topmast. "It worked, sir, the deck is beginning to burn."

"Mr Salmon, fire the rest and try and space them apart."

That was quickly done and soon smoke and then flames were seen rising up. The gentle breeze fanned the flames which quickly rose higher. Soon the flames touched the tarred shrouds and rapidly consumed them. Some small explosions were heard, probably from some ready use powder bags stored near the upper deck guns. The fire spread faster and faster and soon all three masts, the sails and yards were aflame.

Suddenly five figures were seen on the quarter deck, waving madly for help but the marine captain, with a face like stone, ordered the marines to fire. "And do it properly, or I'll know the reason why not." The muskets flamed as one and three of the men dropped back out of sight, one fell across the rail with his coat alight and the other simply stood there waiting to be shot. A marine volley soon obliged him and he fell back into the fire.

"Mr Andrews, I want this ship well away from that fire. It must reach the powder magazine eventually and then I will speak to the men."

That was done and a sullen-faced crew assembled on the gundeck and side decks to hear what he had to say.

"Men, this has been a terrible business but there was no choice. That was a plague ship and if we had tried to save those men the disease would have been transferred to this ship with consequences you can imagine and which I couldn't risk. That is all."

The French ship was now alight from stem to stern and not long after that the powder magazine on the burning ship exploded. Burning timber was scattered all round but the *Lord Stevenage* was well to windward and far enough away to miss it.

All watched silently because no seaman likes to see a ship burning. Finally Merriman ordered that the hulk should be finished off with gunfire. A full broadside to the waterline had the desired effect and the still burning remains disappeared beneath the waves with much hissing and steam as cold water reached the burning timbers. All that was left were some floating, smouldering timbers and some scorched and burned bodies floating on the surface.

"Gentlemen, I believe we have completed our orders," said Merriman. "We shall return to Copenhagen and the fleet. Mr Henderson, set a course for Copenhagen."

Chapter Twenty

Report to Admiral Nelson

Three days later many sails appeared to the south of them and two frigates hastened over to investigate what ship approached. Signals quickly established the *Lord Stevenage's* identity and, as they closed on the fleet, another signal from the flagship ordered Merriman to come aboard. All the ships hove to and all captains were called to the flagship which was flying a blue Admiral's flag at the fore masthead.

Merriman's boat waited while more senior officers boarded. Then, as he climbed on to the deck to the usual sound of the bos'n's whistles and salutes from the marines, a flag lieutenant met him and whispered in his ear that it was Nelson below and he had been made a Viscount and Rear-Admiral of the Blue. He then escorted Merriman below to the Admiral's quarters, where all the other captains were gathered. Merriman was astonished to meet Admiral Nelson instead of Admiral Parker as he had expected.

Nelson rose to his feet when Merriman entered the cabin. "It's a pleasure to meet you again, Captain Merriman. Gentlemen, Captain Merriman is the man who made such a good report about, and charts of the defences of Copenhagen."

There were murmurs of congratulation and handshakes before Nelson said, "Sit down, gentlemen, you will join me in a glass of claret, I know." When all were seated with a glass of claret in hand, Nelson looked round them all and said, "Now then, gentlemen, most of you know one another but you may not know Captain Merriman. I sent Captain Merriman in his frigate *Lord Stevenage* together with two fast sloops to investigate in the eastern Baltic and report back to me the condition of the Russian fleet, with the results that you know. Captain Merriman, your two sloops returned with your reports, but that was weeks ago. Probably by now the Russian fleet will not be icebound, which is why we are here now. Another thing, Captain, you were tasked with keeping an eye open for the reported French warship loose in the Baltic, did you find it?"

"Yes, my lord, I did, but first may I congratulate you on your preferment to the Blue. Indeed, we found that French ship, but you need to worry about her no longer." Merriman recounted how they had found the ship drifting with no sails set properly. "I approached slowly and with great care to windward but there was no sign of life. Then the lookout reported bodies lying all over the deck. I sent Doctor McBride aloft to see what he could make of it and he said that from what he could see it was a plague ship. Many of the bodies were naked and covered in sores."

There were cries of horror from the assembled captains and remarks such as, "You didn't board it, I hope?" and, "Did you sink it?" as well as, "What did you do?"

"I set fire to it, gentlemen. My gunner, a most resourceful man, devised a burning projectile to be fired from a carronade. Several were fired to land on the ship's deck and they started fires which quickly spread until she was burning from end to end."

"Were there any living men left on that ship, Captain?" asked one of the group.

"Yes, sir," replied Merriman. "There may have been some below but if so they were most certainly affected and I couldn't risk sending anybody aboard to find out before setting light to it. Five men appeared on her quarterdeck waving for help but I ordered the marines to shoot them. Again I couldn't risk bringing them aboard my ship. I don't know what else I could have done and I have my written report here, Admiral. I trust you will approve."

"Certainly I do, Captain, what else could you do? Now, whilst you have been away we have learned that as you said in your report, the Tsar of Russia, Paul, has died. That has been confirmed from several sources. Also the League of Armed Neutrality has been abandoned, at least for now. The fleet will now be sailing back to Copenhagen. Another item, Captain, Admiral Parker has been recalled and I am now the Commander-in-Chief of the entire Baltic Fleet."

"Congratulations again, m'lord," said Merriman. "May I ask, what are my orders now?"

"You will come back to Copenhagen with us, Captain. A naval ship should have arrived by now from London with more orders and letters for us all."

Once back in Copenhagen, with the fleet safely anchored in or near the harbour, Merriman felt able to relax below until the marine sentry banged his musket on the deck and announced, "Midshipman Edwards, sir." Edwards duly appeared and reported, "Signal from Flag, sir, our number and captain to go aboard. Your cox'n, Mr Matthews, is getting your boat ready, sir."

Merriman was pleased to see that the boy was no longer nervous but spoke with much more confidence. *That boy might make a good officer in a few years,* mused Merriman as he was hastily dressing in his best uniform. Above decks he climbed down into his gig to the usual ceremony and the boat pushed off. In only a few minutes he was climbing the flagship's side, aided by the white handropes held by the sideboys and then raising his hat as the usual ceremony was observed.

Lord Nelson met him with a smile. "Ah, Merriman, do sit down and have a glass of claret with me. It's not as good as the claret I tasted aboard your ship but it is at least drinkable. Now, the reason for calling you over is that I have received orders for you from the Admiralty. You are to return to Portsmouth without delay, what for I cannot tell you. You can take copies of my reports with you. Do you need to take on any fresh stores and water before you go?"

"Only some fresh vegetables if possible, m'lord. My ship has none left. As for water, we may have sufficient as the men don't need as much to drink in these cold conditions but as your lordship knows, it is always well to stock up when you can, so water and vegetables are needed, sir."

"Good, see my flag lieutenant as you leave. He will arrange it all." Nelson broke off and shouted for his secretary. "There are some letters for your ship, Captain."

The man entered clutching a leathern wallet containing the latest letters which doubtless were already months old and Merriman took his leave. The flag lieutenant was waiting and confirmed that the necessary items would be sent off to the *Lord Stevenage* immediately. It was quickly done and the ship made ready to depart. Merriman wrote a brief note to the Admiral and sent it and a bottle of his best claret to the Flagship.

Chapter Twenty-One

Return to Admiralty bearing Nelson's reports

After an uneventful voyage, *Lord Stevenage* nosed slowly into Portsmouth harbour to the usual noise of the signal guns. They anchored as indicated by the Harbourmaster's boat. As he had done so many times, Merriman stood ready in his best uniform, freshly brushed and pressed by his servant Peters, his sword polished and gleaming and with his own and Lord Nelson's reports ready to take ashore.

On arrival at the Naval offices, he told a worried-looking lieutenant who he was and prepared himself for the usual wait. The lieutenant was soon back and told Merriman that Admiral Fitzherbert would see him in a few minutes. Only a short moment elapsed before he was called in, to the obvious disapproval of the officers already waiting.

"Good to see you again, Captain, welcome. We knew you were coming. That telegraph system is wonderful, don't you think? Now sit down and tell me all about what you have been up to in the Baltic." The Admiral seemed to say all that without once drawing breath, before shouting for his Flag Lieutenant to bring drinks.

"Brandy or wine, sir?" asked the man. Merriman chose wine and the Admiral chose brandy. As the lieutenant made to take the tray of bottles away, the Admiral said, "Leave it, Prudhoe. We may need more."

Merriman launched into his account of what had occurred in the Baltic, the battle of Copenhagen, the search for the Russian fleet, and the plague ship.

"My God, a plague ship, how did you deal with that?" cried Fitzherbert. Of course Merriman told the Admiral all that had happened and what he had done. "That was well done, Captain, but why did you not shoot at it first?"

"Well, sir, I thought there was something wrong. She wasn't sailing, just drifting and no guns run out, indeed her portlids were closed. Naturally I chose to approach on the windward side and my lookout aloft reported the bodies on the deck so I kept well clear. It's all in my written report for you, sir, and I have copies for the Admiralty in London."

"Good, very good. Your friend Mr Grahame knows you are here and the expense of a post-chaise to take you to London has been allowed. You will meet Grahame at the Admiralty. Quite what the hurry is I don't know, so collect what you need from your ship and leave your First Lieutenant in command. I know he is a very capable man and he can deal with all the paperwork involved with the dockyard and such, so I suggest that you go back aboard to collect what you need, then come back here where your carriage will be waiting."

The journey to London was fast and uncomfortable, but Merriman enjoyed seeing the lush countryside as the coach passed through the rolling hills of the Downs and the Devil's Punchbowl. He gazed out at all the sleepy villages they passed through, stopping at regular intervals for fresh horses. Then they were clattering through Esher and finally over the Thames at Putney and so into London. It was late and full dark by then, so Merriman directed the postilion to drop him and his cases off at the same hotel he stayed at last time he had to report to the Admiralty.

The following morning, with his best uniform again freshly pressed and brushed, he presented himself early at the Admiralty and asked that Admiral Edwards be told of his arrival. The lieutenant he spoke to informed him that the Admiral was not yet present but would be informed as soon as he arrived. In the event Merriman had no more than an hour to wait although the waiting room steadily filled up with more officers, some of whom Merriman knew. Then the lieutenant appeared and told Merriman that Admiral Edwards would see him now.

As Merriman entered the well-remembered room with its huge mahogany table in the centre, he was surprised to find that the Admiral was not alone. Standing by one of the windows was Mr Grahame from the Treasury, who had requested Merriman's services in the past. Striding forward, Grahame clasped hands with Merriman, saying, "It's good to see you again, James, and to see that you are well."

"Thank you, sir. I am glad to see you again too."

The Admiral interrupted. "Gentlemen, please be seated. Captain Merriman, I see that you have several reports with you, surely not all yours?"

"No, Sir David, they are mostly from Lord Nelson who asked me to deliver them, not knowing how soon he could bring them in person." Merriman watched while the Admiral was sorting out the reports and was startled to observe that he was really an old man now who was looking weary and had more wrinkles on his face than he had two years ago. The Admiral had been a friend of Merriman's father when they had been young lieutenants together at the start of their careers and Merriman was sorry to see his decline.

"Mr Grahame, perhaps you would be kind enough to tell the Captain what events are unfolding here." The Admiral coughed and reached for a glass of water before going on, "You see, Captain, that damned man over the Channel is trying to negotiate a peace treaty with us and I for one don't trust him." He intimated to Grahame that he should continue.

"That is true, James. From all that we can learn we think it is only Napoleon's ruse to give him time to gather his forces together, both on land and sea, before declaring war again. Our good friend Mr Pitt is out of office now due to ill health. The current Prime Minister is a Henry Addington, a weak man preferring to give way to the French rather than stand up for Britain as Mr Pitt would do. He wants to reduce the number of ships to save payment to the men. The army is being reduced as well."

Merriman frowned.

"The preliminary documents are expected to be signed in October and ratified by March next year but, as Sir David says, we can't trust him. Some of his demands are that we return French possessions in the Caribbean and let him have Malta, the crossroads of the Mediterranean. This must not be allowed to happen. We can let him have one or two of the smaller islands in the West Indies but not Malta, it is too important to us. So you see, James, I am going to send you off on another mission to find out what the feelings are about this of the people of Malta, Italy and other places out there currently being held to us by treaty."

"Will you be coming with me, sir? I mean I am no agent or spy, indeed all I did was to take you where you wished to go. You are the one who went ashore to meet your agents."

"No, I shall not be with you this time, James. As I told you when we last met, your patron Lord Stevenage is not well, indeed I think he will not live much longer, so I have been appointed his successor at the Treasury, with all that that entails. Anyway, we have much to discuss about your next mission but I can tell you that one of my most trusted agents will go with you. Now, Admiral, I think we should leave you. I know that you are a very busy man. My discussions with the Captain can wait until we are at the Treasury."

"Very well, Mr Grahame. Good fortune go with you, Captain, I don't think we shall meet again. Mr Grahame has told me about some of what he has prepared for you."

They shook hands and Merriman and Grahame left. Once outside, Grahame said, "I have a carriage waiting and I have a surprise waiting for you. First we must go to your hotel and collect your belongings and then we are going elsewhere."

"Where are we going?" asked a bewildered Merriman apprehensively as he climbed into the carriage. Despite all the news he'd received, he was not too bewildered to notice the musket propped up by the coachman and the brace of pistols in pockets in the doors.

Grahame spotted that Merriman had seen the weapons and said quietly, "There could well be rioting in the streets before the week is out. So many men are coming home from the fleet and the army with no work waiting for them, and the factories that make uniforms and muskets and all the equipment for war are laying men off as well."

Chapter Twenty-Two

The King honours Merriman

The carriage made its way through the crowded streets then drew up at steps which led up to an imposing house, one in a terrace of houses. "Here we are, James. Follow me," Grahame said. Turning to the coachman he added, "Take it round to the mews, Belton. I don't think we shall need it again today."

Climbing the well-scrubbed steps to a solid, green painted front door sporting gleaming brasswork, Merriman was surprised when it was opened by a smart, liveried and bewigged footman who stood aside and bowed them in.

Merriman's bewilderment was increased by the sight of the figure standing by one of the big doors leading off the hall. "By the gods, Helen. Is that really you?" he cried excitedly.

"Yes, James, it really is me," she said and rushed forward into his arms.

The footman closed the door and pretended to be looking elsewhere with an expressionless face while Grahame removed his coat with a big smile on his face. "That is the surprise I promised you, James. Happy now?"

"Oh yes, sir, I mean Laurence. How did you manage this?" said Merriman looking down onto his wife's smiling face. "However you did it, it is wonderful. I thought I would have to wait to see her until I got home again. Thank you."

"Oh, it wasn't all my doing. Come into the big room over here, there is someone else I want you to meet."

That someone was no other than Sir William D'Ablay, the fourth Lord Stevenage who had been responsible for Merriman's advancement and promotion.

"My lord," cried Merriman in surprise. "Mr Grahame told me that you are not well. I had imagined you to be at your country house, not in the smells and noise of London."

"I have been, James, but I had to come to London to see to one or two matters. This is my house and, expecting you to be home soon, I arranged for the delightful Helen to come and stay to keep an old man company until you arrived. I tell you, James, if I were forty years younger you would have your work cut out to keep hold of her, I promise you."

Lord Stevenage turned to Helen and said, "Helen, my dear, are you going to show your husband the next surprise?"

She opened the door and called out, "Annie, come here."

Annie, once Merriman's mother's friend and housekeeper, came into the room carrying a child little more than a baby and holding a little boy of some three years old by the hand. She curtsied to the gentlemen and said, "Master James, don't look so bewildered. These two are yours."

Helen took the baby in her arms and, turning to Merriman, she said, "Meet your new daughter, James. I called her Mary Anne after your mother, I hope you approve."

"How could I not, my dear! Has she been christened yet?"

"Yes, James, like her brother in the local church."

Lord Stevenage interrupted. "I would have liked to be her godfather, James. Helen did ask me but I was too ill to travel."

Merriman became conscious of a tiny figure standing next to him, thumb in mouth, tugging at his breeches. "And this fine boy must be my son, Robert," said Merriman, lifting the boy up into his arms.

The child squealed with delight and reached out to tug at one of the golden epaulettes in front of him. That old trick of lifting the child into the air and then pretending to drop him called forth more squeals of delight. With Helen, his children and his friends around him, Merriman had never felt happier.

"I am delighted to see you all reunited, James, but I am tired now and need to rest. We all have a big day tomorrow and I don't want to miss it," said Lord Stevenage. Annie called for his valet and footman and they gently lifted the old man from his chair and supported him as he walked out of the room.

There was silence for a moment before Merriman said, "I am sad to see him like this, so different from the tall man with a bloody sword I saved all those years ago when his ship was attacked by corsairs off the west coast of Africa." Annie had disappeared with the two children and Merriman continued, "What did he mean by a big day tomorrow?"

Both Helen and Grahame smiled and Helen said, "You will find out tomorrow, James. Now you must be hungry, dinner is being served in the other room so let us eat."

A fine meal it was, the conversation flowed, but for all his subtle questioning Merriman learned nothing about what would happen the next day. After the meal, Grahame excused himself saying only, "I'll leave you two alone now. Don't forget the big day tomorrow so try and get a bit of sleep." He winked at Merriman and said, "Don't want you yawning at the wrong time, do we?"

James and Helen were soon into bed and, after vigorous lovemaking, they fell asleep in the early hours of the morning. A light knock on the door wakened them and, at Helen's call, a maid entered carrying a tray with their breakfast. "Good morning, sir, ma'am," she said. "Your clothes are being made ready for your big day."

She scuttled out and Merriman said crossly, "Even the servants know what is to happen today, but I'm not allowed to know, Helen. Why is that?"

"You will find out soon enough, James, so don't fret," said Helen sweetly.

Downstairs they found Mr Grahame and Lord Stevenage waiting for them. Lord Stevenage was beautifully dressed in elegant clothing with several ribbons and orders across his breast including the prestigious Order of the Garter. Mr Grahame was simply dressed in dark clothing and both of them greeted Merriman warmly. Helen made her entrance a few minutes later and all stood speechless for a moment before Lord Stevenage bowed deeply and said, "You are looking radiant this morning, my dear. My God, James, you are a lucky man to have such a wife."

"Thank you, my lord," she said, curtseying to him.

Merriman looked at her in awe. Helen was dressed in a new gown which he had not seen before. She wore diamonds sparkling on her breast and neck, and a silk shawl draped round her shoulders, the colour of which matched her eyes.

"Are we all ready then?" asked his Lordship. "Then we must be off. Perhaps you will give me your arm, James?"

A footman opened the front door and, with Merriman and the footman assisting, Stevenage descended the steps and entered his waiting carriage. When all were seated, another footman folded the step and closed the door before climbing up behind to join another footman at the back of the carriage.

"Will nobody tell me where we are going?" asked Merriman.

Grahame winked and said, "Patience, James. You will know soon enough."

The carriage made its slow way through the streets and Merriman, not knowing much about London, had to confess that he was lost.

"We are nearly there now, James," said his Lordship as the carriage turned into a fine pair of gates and up a short driveway to a big house. There were soldiers on guard at the gates and by the door. As they descended from the carriage, a pompous, liveried footman greeted them. "Follow me, my lord, if you will," he said. They all followed him into a modest sized hall with liveried footmen standing at every door.

"What is this place, sir?" Merriman whispered to his patron as he supported him.

"This is Kew Palace, James. You are going to meet the King at a levee."

Poor Merriman barely had time to digest the fact before a pair of double doors were opened and they were ushered into a huge room ablaze with the light of hundreds of candles and lamps. A blast of hot air greeted them as they stepped inside and Merriman immediately felt sweat running down his back. A bewigged official banged the butt of his heavy cane on the floor and bawled, "Sir William D'Ablay, Lord Stevenage, Mr Grahame and Captain Merriman and his lady."

It took a few minutes for the noise to die down and Merriman realised he was faced by a crowd of people. The blue and gold of naval officers was there, the red coats of the army as well as many men in elegant clothing, knee breeches and silk stockings, fancy waistcoats and embroidered coats sporting ribbons and medals in profusion. Ladies were there in plenty, wearing gorgeous gowns of silk and lace and heavily embroidered fabrics, with very revealing necklines and jewels gleaming, their bold and interesting eyes looking at him over their fans.

The air was heavy with the scent of perfumes and Merriman's first thought was a longing for fresh air. A passageway appeared before them. Lord Stevenage released Merriman's arm and drew himself up to his full height before leading the way forward and bowing to a man who Merriman realised must be King George.

"Ah, Sir William, I'm pleased to see you here again," the king said. "Please introduce your friends."

"Yes, sire, this is Mr Grahame from the Treasury, whom you know, and Captain James Merriman and his lady."

Helen curtseyed deeply as the King said, "You are all welcome. So you are the famous Captain Merriman, are you, the scourge of Indian pirates and the French? My friend Sir William has told me all about you and your exploits, as have some of my Admirals."

In a daze Merriman realised a red carpet was being laid out by footmen and Sir William whispered, "Kneel, James, now." He did so, desperately trying not to tangle his legs with his sword and keeping his head bowed. Then the King tapped him on both shoulders with a sword passed to him and said, "Rise, Sir James, and we are well pleased with you and your deeds at sea."

"Thank you, sire, for the honour," Merriman said, rising to his feet and backing away.

"I honour you with a great deal of pleasure, Sir James, for all that you have done for this country," said the King with a smile.

The next to kneel was Grahame. He too was tapped on the shoulders with the King's sword. "Rise, Sir Laurence," said the King. "I am well aware of the great service you have done for this country. Much of it must perforce remain secret but I know thanks to Lord Stevenage here. Am I not right, Sir William?"

"Indeed, sire, you are, as well as knowing about Sir James' deeds which I told you of."

"Quite right, William. I only wish I had more time to hear more about these gentlemen's' deeds, but duty awaits." The King turned to Helen who had been watching with a happy expression on her face. He took her hand "You are welcome, Lady Helen. You are fortunate to have such a distinguished officer for your husband." Helen curtsied but before she could speak the King turned away to speak with other men who were trying to catch his eye.

"Now is the time to leave, James," said Sir William quietly. "Back away a few steps then we shall go."

As they neared the entrance hall, Merriman felt His Lordship clutch at his arm to steady himself and, with Helen supporting him also, he managed to walk a little further. Grahame had moved ahead to call for the carriage and when they had all climbed in Sir William fell back on his seat breathing a big sigh.

"I'm glad that is over. I don't know how I managed to stand for so long."

"Determination, my lord, of which I know you have in plenty," replied Grahame.

"Thank you, Laurence, thank you. Now please see me home before the two of you go to your next important appointment."

"Next important appointment?" echoed Merriman. "What could be more important than what has just happened?"

His Lordship smiled weakly and waved his hand. "You will soon find out, James."

On arrival at the town house, the three of them clustered round him and, with the help of two footmen, he was carried up to his bedroom where his valet Phillips met him and chided him, "My lord, you have being doing too much again. I warned you and the doctor advised against it you know." He turned to the rest of them saying, "Please leave now. I can do all that is needed and Perkins will help me." He indicated the footman standing by the door then shooed them out and closed the door behind them.

"A good man, that valet," said Grahame as they went downstairs. "Been with Sir William since long before I met him. Now, James, we have been offered the use of the carriage for your next appointment and we must be off if we are not to be late."

As the carriage clattered along through the rough streets and smells of the city, Merriman asked no more questions. He was too amazed by the morning's events, and he simply sat there clutching Helen's hand, as ready as he could be for what was to happen next. Obviously the coachman had been told where to go because, with no instructions from Grahame, he eventually turned into Leadenhall Street and drew to a halt in front of the six columned portico of East India House. One of their footmen assisted them to alight and as they approached the door, it was opened by two footmen dressed in sober black who asked their names. "Sir James Merriman and Lady Merriman and I am Sir Laurence Graham. We are expected, I believe."

"Yes, Sir Laurence, indeed you are. Please follow me," said one of the footmen.

The man led them to a huge mahogany door, knocked on it, opened it and repeated, "Sir James and Lady Merriman and Sir Laurence Grahame, gentlemen," before he withdrew and closed the door behind him. There were perhaps twenty well-dressed men in the room, all turning to smile at them. One man introduced himself as the Governor of the Court of Directors and proceeded to introduce the others present.

"I am aware that you won't remember most of our names," he said, "but we all know that the Company is indebted to you both for your actions in India. Governor Duncan sent a report by one of our fastest Indiamen of all that you both did and we are delighted, Sir James, to present you with this as a token of our appreciation." He turned and picked up a gleaming sword from the table behind him. "You will see that the blade is finely engraved as is the scabbard."

Merriman accepted the weapon and managed to stammer out his thanks before the Governor picked up a mahogany box and presented it to Grahame. "For you, Sir Laurence, for the same reason. Go on, man, open it. It won't bite."

Grahame opened the box to reveal a pair of beautifully wrought flintlock pistols with mahogany grips and with engraving along the barrel.

"Thank you, gentlemen, this is a surprise. I knew I was bringing Sir James here for you to present him with the sword, but I had no idea that I would be given this gift as well."

The other men crowded round to congratulate them, drinks were provided and the conversation became louder. Many of the men approached Helen and spoke to her. The conversation continued for quite a long time before Helen touched James on the arm and whispered, "If we can leave here, James, we should go and see how Lord Stevenage is."

"Of course, you are right, my dear." Merriman turned to his friend and spoke quietly, "Laurence, can we be excused? We should go and see Sir William."

"Yes of course, James. Gentlemen, may I have your attention?" Grahame called loudly and in the sudden silence he explained why they had to leave so soon.

"Of course you should go. Sir William is a good friend of mine and I had wondered why he did not come here with you," said the Governor. "Go, and tell him we all wish him well."

They left with many messages of goodwill ringing in their ears and though back in the carriage they all sat in silence, almost overwhelmed by what had happened. At Sir William's town house they were met by a worried Phillips, the valet, who told them that His Lordship was sleeping. "The doctor has given him something to make him sleep but said he should not be disturbed before morning."

They slept fitfully that night and while they were taking breakfast at about eight o' clock the valet interrupted them. He announced that his Lordship wished to see them. They found Lord Stevenage sitting up in bed, supported by a mound of pillows. His face seemed more lined than before but as they neared his bed he opened his eyes. To Merriman they seemed to be as bright, stern and commanding as they had been so long ago when first they met. But it was soon evident that he was not the same man as of old, his voice was weak and trembling and his veined hands lying on the coverlet were shaking.

He beckoned them closer and said, "My good friends, I have decided to be taken back to my place in the country and I would like you, James and Helen, to go with me. Laurence, you must stay in London, you will be busier than ever with that imbecile Addington discharging so many troops and sailors. There will be riots in the streets, I'm sure, and I can no longer help."

"Don't worry, sir, you have trained me well and I know what I have to do."

"You are a good man, Laurence. I'm sorry I am stuck here and I fear that you will not see me again in this world."

Grahame took hold of his mentor's hand. "Oh you will, sir, you will. I'll visit as often as I can," replied Grahame brokenly.

"No, Laurence, you won't. I know I haven't got long in this world, but you have much before you that needs a firm hand on the reins. So goodbye, my dear friend. Leave us now."

Grahame gave a deep sob and, as he turned away, Merriman and Helen saw the tears running down his face. Sir William kept his eyes closed for a moment or two before he held out his hands to them and said, "Cheer up you two, I'm not dead yet. I've a few more days left in me still. As I said, I want you to come with me to the country. You and my valet can look after me and I want to see the look on your face when you see your new estate. As for me, I want to see again the home where my wife and I were so happy before we lost our young son."

He appeared to fall asleep before Helen said, "We shall be with you, sir, all the way." At that he smiled and feebly said, "Thank you, my dear."

Chapter Twenty-Three

Merriman travels with Lord Stevenage

The coach they travelled in was not the usual one but a larger, heavier one with extra horses to pull it. It was quite spacious and James and Helen occupied one bench seat with Phillips the valet while Sir William lay opposite to them on the other seat. In spite of the bumps and rumblings of the carriage, he seemed to sleep quite well and when they reached an inn on the first night he was able to walk a little with their help.

A second smaller carriage carried Annie and the two children with one of Sir William's older maids. Phillips insisted on helping Sir William to bed after a simple meal of hot milk and biscuit, after which then valet came down to join them in the inn's small dining room. He sat quietly for a short while saying nothing before he slumped forward with a groan and put his face in his hands. Helen and James moved to him and endeavoured to comfort him but he sobbed uncontrollably. Eventually he pulled himself together and spoke.

"I'm sorry for that pathetic display, Sir James and your Ladyship. I have been with Sir William for over thirty years and I can't believe the end is near. If only I could do something."

"You have been his valet and more for all that time and I'm sure his friend also. No man could do more," said Helen.

"Yes, I was," Phillips said. "He was my entire life. He raised me from being a miserable stable boy and showed me a whole new world in his house. I think that sometimes he saw me as a replacement for his dead son, but our relationship never went beyond that." He paused, then said, "What will I do when he is gone?"

"We know that you are amply provided for under his will but have you no family or relations you could go to?" asked Merriman.

Phillips shook his head sadly. "No, sir, nobody now. My sister died some years ago and she was my only close relative. Anyway, money can't replace him in my life." He sat quietly for a while then he roused himself and said, "I must go up to him now and see if I can do anything for him Thank you for your kindness."

"Poor man. He must feel lost now and will no longer have a focus for his life," said Helen. "What can we do, James?"

"I don't know," he replied, "but we must discuss it some more."

The next day dawned bright and clear and overnight rain had softened some of the mud in the road so that the next two days travelling was more comfortable. Sir William even sat upright for a time and chatted with his companions. He seemed quite cheerful but they knew it was but a brief recovery. Eventually the afternoon arrived when the carriage arrived at the gates into the estate. From there a man was sent on a horse to warn the house staff that their Lord was nearly home.

The carriage trundled up the driveway which must have been at least a mile long and then, on rounding a clump of stately oaks, the house came into view beyond a large lake. It was an old Tudor building with a new frontage and extension and looked very grand. A church steeple showed over a large patch of woodland.

Sir William pointed to it and said, "That church is where all my family are buried. I will follow them soon." Brushing off their objections, he continued looking eagerly about him, smiled and pointed to the lake, "That is where I used to swim with my father when I was a boy and I even had a boat there. My grandfather had those trees planted before I was born. On the other side of the lake is an arbour where my dear wife used to sit and watch the deer we have on the estate... Ah memories, memories. I love this place."

The carriage pulled to a halt in front of the front door where all the estate staff were grouped on either side of the steps. As Sir William was helped from the carriage and assisted to climb the steps by James and Helen, all the staff either bowed or curtseyed. At the top of the steps, a man in a magnificently frogged coat came forward and said, "Welcome home, my lord. All is well."

Sir William nodded to him, saying, "Thank you, Mr Gordon, and thank you all. My friends are Sir James and Lady Merriman; you will extend to them all the hospitality of this house. Their children can be in the old nursery. Now I must rest before I look round the house again."

"Yes, my lord. We shall look after them all, have no fear about that."

Phillips and a footman took over the care of Sir William and carried him upstairs while James and Helen entered the great entrance hall where they looked round in amazement. They had thought that their own mansion at Burton was a fine house but it seemed to pale into insignificance when they saw all of the fine pictures on the walls and the statues and carvings placed in alcoves and round the walls. A discreet cough behind them brought them back to reality. It was Mr Gordon who said, "Excuse me, sir. Your luggage has been taken to your rooms and hot water will be brought up to you shortly. You will find a maid and valet waiting up there. Now if you would follow me?"

He led them slowly up a magnificent polished oak staircase to the next floor where he opened a big door into a huge suite of rooms, a bedroom with a huge four-poster bed, a lounge and dressing rooms.

They crossed to the window and saw a magnificent view of the lake. Mr Gordon coughed quietly and said, "Lady Merriman and Sir, this was Lady Stevenage's room, her favourite. Sir William sent word in advance that you were to have these rooms when you arrived. They have been kept clean and tidy but nobody else has slept here since she died so many years ago. The housekeeper Miss Trimshaw has seen to it that a fire has been lit on cold and damp days."

"Thank you, Mr Gordon. Have the maid and valet sent in right away with the hot water. We shall have our clothes unpacked and wash and change and then look in on Sir William if he can receive visitors," said Helen.

"Very good, Lady Helen. If you will go down to the small dining room when you are ready. A meal will have been made ready for you. Mr Phillips will join you and let you know if Sir William is able to see you."

Later, they ate a modest but delicious meal with two bewigged footmen serving the food and wine. Then Mr Phillips appeared and told them that His Lordship was sleeping and would they wait until tomorrow to see him. They spent the next two hours walking round the magnificent rooms on the ground floor and then went up to find the nursery to find the two children and Annie, after which, tired out, they went to bed.

Chapter Twenty-Five

Death of Lord Stevenage

Merriman and his wife slept well and were roused by a knock on the door. The maid entered carrying a tray of tea which she put down on a small table, curtseyed and then drew the curtains to reveal bright sunlight and a blue sky above. The couple took great care to dress well, with the valet and maid helping, indeed the valet shaved Merriman and told him that they would find breakfast ready in the small dining room. Neither of them felt like eating much and, as soon as they finished, Phillips told them that his master was weaker and wanted to see them right away.

When they entered the bedroom they found Sir William lying back, supported by a mound of pillows. Phillips, Mr Gordon and a doctor were standing by the bed but Sir William waved them away and held out his hands to beckon Merriman and his wife to join him. He smiled weakly and drew them nearer to him.

"James… James and Helen, I know I'm dying but don't grieve for me. You are my only family now and I have often thought of you, James, as the son I lost so long ago. And, Helen, your beauty has made an old man very happy."

Helen sniffed and reached out to take his hand.

"Admiral Edwards and I have done all we can for you, James. You are now a knight of the realm, richly deserved, and I am sure you will climb higher as the years pass. And now I would like to see my young godson for the last time and little Mary Ann too. Will you fetch them to me please, Helen? I think they may be outside the door with Annie."

The children were brought in and both looked at him with big round eyes as he took one hand of each of them and said, "God bless you both my dears."

His eyes closed and Helen told Annie to take the children out of the room. He opened his eyes again and whispered, "I enjoyed that. It was as though they were my own..."

His eyes closed for the last time and it was all over. Helen burst into tears and Merriman himself was not unaffected. The doctor felt for a pulse but shook his head and drew the sheet over the dead man's face. Poor Phillips stood there with tears running down his face and even Gordon's eyes were moist.

Merriman placed an arm around his wife's shoulders. "Come, my dear," he said. "We can do nothing for him now."

He beckoned to both Phillips and Gordon to go with them and whispered to Gordon that he must speak to the house staff right away.

"They are all waiting in the hall, Sir James. They all know what has happened and you can speak to them from the balcony overlooking the hall."

In the hall below housemaids, footmen, gardeners and men from the stables were waiting, all bareheaded and many of the women sobbing quietly into their aprons. Merriman looked at them for a few moments then said, with a catch in his voice, "I'm sure that you all know that Sir William has died. He was a fine man and a gentleman and he will be sadly missed both by us all here and by many of his friends and colleagues in London. What you may not know is that His Lordship left all his property to me and so now this fine hall and all in it is mine. But I must assure you that there will be no changes made and you all can remain here. My wife and I shall stay for the funeral but then we shall have to leave, but we shall be back. I am certain that you will look after everything as you would if His Lordship was still with us. Thank you all."

The funeral took place on a bright sunny morning a week later and, as the cortege left the great house on its way to the church, Merriman was surprised at the number of country folk waiting with all the house staff. As they walked into the church, the ever present Gordon whispered in Merriman's ear, "Everyone loved him, Sir James. You don't know them but there are people here from all over the estate and the village to pay their respects."

Back at the house, Merriman called Mr Gordon into the small dining room and motioned to him to shut the door. "Mr Gordon, as you know my wife and I must leave. I am a serving sea officer and must go to the Admiralty as soon as I can and Lady Helen and the children will go home. But we shall be back and meanwhile I leave the estate and house in the care of yourself, Miss Trimshaw the housekeeper, and the estate bailiffs. I cannot say for certain how long it will be before we are back again but His Lordship assured me that all of you are well provided for in his will and should stay here for the foreseeable future."

"Thank you, Sir James. Rest assured, your house will be well cared for. I'm sure that nobody would wish to leave."

"Very good, Mr Gordon. We shall leave at first light in the morning and we shall have to use two of the carriages, the big one to carry my wife and our children and their nurse and all the luggage. See to all of that if you will, Mr Gordon. After they are delivered home, the coachman and footmen can return here if they wish. I will need a small carriage to take me to London." Merriman offered his hand and shook hands with the man who said, "Thank you, Sir James. I will arrange everything."

The following morning, as the family prepared to leave, they found the entire staff waiting for them on the steps. The men bowed and the women curtseyed and Mr Gordon stepped forward and said, "We wish you a safe journey, Sir, and godspeed."

The staff remained on the steps, waving until the carriages disappeared up the long drive.

Chapter Twenty-Six

New orders to go to South America

Arriving in London before midday, Merriman had himself taken to Lord Stevenage's town house to refresh himself before going to the Admiralty. As he climbed the steps to the front door he had to remind himself that it was his house now. The coachman took the carriage round to the mews to send Merriman's luggage in by the back door. The front door was opened by the same livery-clad footman and Merriman asked him to assemble all the staff in the hall while he waited in the biggest room.

The same footman entered and told him that the staff were in the hall and waiting for him. Merriman looked round them all, some he had seen the last time he was at the house but there were several he had not seen including an elderly man dressed in sombre black who introduced himself as Lord Stevenage's head servant Garfield.

"I apologise for not being here the last time you came, Sir James, but His Lordship sent me on several errands, to the Treasury and the Palace and to the Admiralty. I had to wait for the people his Lordship had given me messages for and I didn't manage to get back here until after you all left, Sir."

"Very well, Mr Garfield. Now I'll speak to the people."

Merriman climbed up three steps of the fine staircase so that all could see him and began, "I don't know if word has reached you yet but I am sorry to have to tell you that Sir William is dead." He paused as the news was received by the staff. Some of the women burst into tears and all looked shocked.

"I am sorry to have to bring you the sad news but I was among those at his bedside as he died, peacefully and happy. The funeral was two days ago. I expect that you will all be wondering what is going to happen to you now but I must tell you that Sir William left this house and his country estate to me in his will. I am a serving sea officer and will be away for long periods of time so I do not intend to make any changes here. I trust that you will all care for this house as you were doing when His Lordship was alive. Mr Garfield, I leave it in your hands. Now I have to go to the Admiralty so I must freshen up and change."

"Thank you, Sir James. We shall look after everything for you. Your luggage has been sent up to the rooms you occupied last time you were here and I will send up some hot water immediately."

Half an hour later, dressed in his best uniform, Merriman came downstairs to find Mr Garfield and the maids and footmen waiting for him. "I have taken the liberty of having your carriage brought round, Sir James. It is waiting outside."

"Thank you. I don't know what time I shall be back as that depends on orders I will hear at the Admiralty."

"Yes, sir. The people here asked me to wish you well wherever the Navy sends you."

Touched, Merriman looked round at them, smiled and, as the footman opened the door, they all bowed or curtseyed to him.

At the Admiralty he asked the same harried lieutenant to tell Admiral Sir David Edwards that he was here.

"I'm sorry, sir, but I can't. Sir David died last week. His place has been taken by Admiral Sir Henry Goodwin, sir. We have been expecting you since Sir Laurence Grahame told us last week that you would be here soon. Please follow me, Sir James, the Admiral told me to bring you in as soon as you arrived."

The lieutenant escorted Merriman to a room he had not been in before and as he was ushered in a rather portly man stood and extended his hand. "Glad to meet you, Captain. Both Lord Stevenage and Sir Laurence Grahame have brought me up to date with your career. You have been very successful, I hear. And how is Lord Stevenage, I heard he was ill?"

"He died last week, Sir Henry. I was there and the funeral was two days ago."

"I feared that might be the case, Captain. Sir Laurence told me that he did not think that he would see His Lordship again. A fine gentleman who served his country well. He will be missed, I'm sure. Now then, sit down, Captain. I sent word to Sir Laurence that you had arrived so he will join us soon. I understand that my predecessor told you that you might be going to Malta on behalf of the Treasury, but that has all changed I believe. You will be going elsewhere, again under orders of the Treasury people as before."

He broke off as a knock sounded on the door and the lieutenant stuck his head in and said, "Sir Laurence is here, sir."

"Well bring him in, man, don't shilly-shally," roared the Admiral.

Sir Laurence duly entered and strode straight to Merriman. "It's good to see you again, James. Word reached me about the loss of Sir William, I'm so sorry I couldn't be there. You were there I know, was his end peaceful?"

"Yes, Laurence, it was. He died quietly and happy, with my family and his valet Phillips and Mr Gordon at his bedside."

"Good. I know he thought of you almost as his son, James, and I'm glad you were there." He turned to the Admiral. "I apologise, Sir Henry. James and I have been through many adventures together but reminiscences must wait for another time. We must tell him what his next adventure will be. May I continue, sir?"

The Admiral nodded and Grahame continued. "You will remember, Captain, that you were told that you would be sent to the Mediterranean, Malta in particular, but that has changed. The Admiralty sent another ship and one of my agents there to find out what we wanted you to find out. You have something much more important to do. You are to go to the east coast of South America with another of the Treasury agents, one George Humphries. Mr Humphries speaks both Spanish and French fluently, and Portuguese also. He is an excellent man in every way; I have every confidence that you will find him an agreeable companion. Perhaps, Admiral, you will tell the Captain the naval details?"

"Thank you, Sir. Captain, as you have been told, you are off to South America, but not alone. That French corvette that you captured has finally been made ready for sea again. It had to wait a long time while several bigger ships were repaired for the Channel fleet which was more urgent. That ship, which has been renamed rather unimaginatively as *The Eagle*, is now to be with us together with another ship, a brig, *The Mayfly*, Lieutenant Stewart in command. Admiral Edwards was most insistent that this voyage should wait for you to return and I know that all three ships are fully manned, stored and provisioned for a long voyage. It only remains to appoint a captain for *The Eagle*. Admiral Edwards suggested that your First Lieutenant, Mr Andrews, should be that man. Do you agree?"

"Indeed, sir, I can think of no one better. He is more than ready for that appointment."

"We thought you would say that, so it will be your pleasant duty to give him these orders and his new epaulette down in Portsmouth. Another officer is waiting in Portsmouth to join your ship and Mr Humphries is already there. Here are the orders for Captain Stewart and, in the interest of haste, you are authorised to go by poste-chaise."

"Thank you, Sir Henry. I must go to Sir William's house in town, which is mine now, to collect my cases and baggage and then I shall be off. I have a carriage waiting outside."

"I shall go with you to the house, James," said Grahame. "I have much more to tell you about the situation in South America."

And so, after intense discussions and a fine meal they went their separate ways.

Chapter Twenty-Seven

Merriman sails for Brazil

Forty eight hours after he reported into the Port Admiral's offices, the post-chaise deposited Merriman and his baggage at the same quayside he knew so well. He gave the post-boy a handsome tip and then looked at the various boatmen clamouring for his attention. He picked the same man who had taken him off previously and quickly the luggage was placed aboard the boat with Merriman sitting in the stern.

"The *Lord Stevenage* is it, sir?" asked the boatman. At Merriman's nod he said, "I remember, sir, but she's not moored where she were, she's further out."

After a hard pull the boat neared his ship and in response to a loud hail, Merriman turned back the shoulder of his boatcloak to reveal one of his epaulettes and the boatman roared out, "Lord Stevenage," leaving no doubt in anyone's mind that it was the Captain coming aboard. Merriman gave the man a good tip on top of his price and climbed aboard to all the expected ceremony of whistles and saluting marines.

All the officers were gathered there to greet him and Lieutenant Andrews said, "Welcome back, sir," to the accompanying greetings of the rest of them.

"It is good to be back, David, gentlemen. As soon as my bags are aboard I will wash and change and then call you all down to my cabin."

Merriman's servant Peters quickly appeared with hot water and began to unpack his belongings.

"Not the best uniform this time, Peters, my normal sea-going rig will do. You can clean up the best uniform in case I have to go to see the Admiral tomorrow."

Washed and changed, he passed the word via the marine sentry that all officers should join him in the great cabin. When they were all settled, he said, "I know without asking that the ship is ready for sea in all respects and I have some news for you at last. We are not going to the Mediterranean as you may have hoped, but to South America."

"Where all those dark eyed senoritas live, sir?" exclaimed Lieutenant Shrigley.

"What do you know about dark eyed senoritas, Alfred? You've never been there."

"No, sir, but one hears stories from old seamen."

"I'm sure you do," said Merriman dryly, calling for Peters to bring some wine. The man had been expecting the call and was there immediately with the bottles and with Tomkins carrying a tray of glasses. When all were served Merriman said, "I also have some sad news, gentlemen. Lord Stevenage, after whom this ship is named, died last week. Some of you, those who were at my wedding, will remember him I'm sure. He was a fine gentleman so please join me in a toast to his memory." They all rose and Merriman lifted his glass and said, "To Sir William D'Ablay, Lord Stevenage."

They all responded "To Lord Stevenage," drained their glasses and then sat down.

"As a result of his death Mr Grahame, whom you will all remember, has been appointed to take his place at the Treasury, so he will not be coming with us this time. Instead we are to have another man instead, a Mr Humphries and I expect that you all will make him welcome. He will take Mr Grahame's cabin. I must also tell you that Mr Grahame is now Sir Laurence Grahame and I am now Sir James Merriman. We went to the palace..." his voice was drowned out by the cheers and applause that broke out at his announcement.

"Congratulations, sir. Well-deserved I know," said Andrews. "Now where is your man, Peters? More wine, we must drink a toast to Sir James."

When the noise and excitement had died down, Merriman said, "Thank you, gentlemen. Now some more news for you, the corvette we captured so long ago as we came back from India, *The Eagle*, will be coming with us, as will the brig *The Mayfly*, with Lieutenant Stewart in command. I am to be the senior officer of the little flotilla, Commodore if you will, and we shall set sail as soon as Mr Humphries and another person come aboard."

"But, sir, *The Eagle* hasn't got a captain yet," said Lieutenant Merryweather.

"Oh, most remiss of me, gentlemen. She does have a new captain." Merriman paused and took a folder off his desk. "The new captain is..." He paused. "Post Captain Andrews!"

Again the cabin erupted in cheers and loud congratulations while Andrews sat there with a surprised expression on his face.

"Come, sir, have you nothing to say?" shouted Lieutenant Shrigley.

"Give him time, gentlemen," said Merriman, waving a new epaulette in front of him.

Andrews stood up slowly, took the new epaulette, cleared his throat and said in the sudden silence, "Thank you all for your congratulations. Did you have anything to do with this, sir?"

"Indeed I did, David. When Admiral Edwards asked me if I could recommend anyone for the post I told him I could think of nobody better. You have my congratulations too, and it is well deserved."

"Put it on, sir, put it on," shouted a midshipman, pointing to the shiny new epaulette. Again all joined in. "Put it on, put it on, put it on," they chanted and cheered when Andrews took off his coat to fix the epaulette and then put his coat back on.

"That will do for now, gentlemen. I would be obliged if you left. Captain Andrews, you will stay for a few minutes."

Everybody wanted to shake Andrews' hand before they left but soon the two men were left alone. Andrews sat down with a bump. "Is this real, sir? I mean it's so sudden I can't take it all in. Post at last. I dreamed of it, of course, but thought I would have to wait longer, what with the news that ships will be laid up."

"It's true enough, David, so you better get used to it. I learned at the Admiralty that all three of the ships are fully stored and manned ready to sail, is that right?"

"Yes, sir. The corvette has new people aboard but I have met the officers and many of the crew and they seem to be sound. In your absence, sir, I took the liberty of checking everything as I did for this ship."

"Good, now here are your orders and commission so you had better get your stuff together and have my cox'n Matthews take you over to your new command to read yourself in. Have a signal sent to the brig, 'Captain to come aboard', at once if you please."

"Aye-aye, sir, and thank you again. If I can make her as good a ship as this, I will be well pleased."

Merriman sat back to consider his next move. He couldn't do anything until Mr Humphries and the new officer came aboard which made him wonder about the new officer and what place he would take in the ranks of the officers. He didn't have to wait long before the thump of the marine sentry's musket on the deck and the sentry called, "Lieutenant Stewart, sir, and a Mr Humphries."

Humphries was a tall, thin man with a lively manner and Merriman took to him at once. The lieutenant was different all together. Short and with a rather dour expression, he was older than his rank seemed to indicate although well experienced, Merriman hoped. He made them both welcome and told them what their orders were. The small talk was interrupted by Midshipman Small who announced, "Signals from Flag, sir. Our number and for the other two, 'Make Sail and good luck'". The boy darted away but was soon back. "Another officer has come aboard, sir. He says he is appointed to us."

"Thank you, Mr Small. Tell him I shall speak to him later. Lieutenant, back to your ship and make ready to sail. I hope to get to know you better over the coming weeks."

"Aye-aye, sir. It will be a pleasure to serve with you, sir," said Stewart with a faint smile.

Three days later the small flotilla was encountering the swells of the Atlantic Ocean as they passed Ushant on the larboard side and, keeping well offshore, they headed for South America and new adventures.

THE END

Author's Notes:

Regrettably the papers covering the years 1802 to 1810 were in too bad a state to decipher at all, indeed some were missing completely. But I will keep at it. It seems that Captain Sir James Merriman with his ship, the frigate *"Lord Stevenage"*, was involved in many actions in South America and must have played a significant part in naval affairs of the time. He must have been involved in many other serious naval actions in those years and acquitted himself very well because there are many mentions of his name in the gazette. Merriman will sail again.

Author Biography
Roger Burnage (1933 to 2015)

Roger Burnage had an eventful life that ultimately led him to pursue his passion for writing. Born and raised in the village of Lymm, Warrington, Cheshire, United Kingdom, he embarked on a journey of adventure and self-discovery.

Roger's life took an intriguing turn when he served in the Royal Air Force (RAF) during his national service. He was stationed in Ceylon, which is now known as Sri Lanka, where he worked as a radio mechanic, handling large transmitters.

After his release from the RAF, Roger went on to work as a draughtsman at Vickers in Manchester. Through dedication and hard work, he eventually climbed the ranks to become a sales engineer. His job involved traveling abroad to places like Scandinavia and India, which exposed him to new cultures and experiences.

It was during this period that Roger Burnage stumbled upon the Hornblower novels by C. S. Forester. The captivating tales of naval adventures ignited a spark of interest in the historical fiction genre within him.

Eventually, Roger settled in North Wales, where he focused on building a business and raising a family. Throughout his professional and personal life, the desire to write for himself never waned. However, it wasn't until retirement that he finally had the time and opportunity to pursue his dream of becoming an author.

Despite facing initial challenges and enduring multiple rejections from publishers and agents, Roger persevered. He refused to give up on his writing aspirations. Even when he underwent open-heart surgery and had an operation for a brain haemorrhage, he continued to work diligently on his craft. Typing away with only two fingers for months on end, he crafted "The Merriman Chronicles."

In 2012, with the support of his youngest son, Robin, Roger self-published his debut novel, "A Certain Threat," on Amazon KDP, making it available in both paperback and Kindle formats. His determination and talent began to bear fruit, as his fan base grew, and book sales remained strong.

More information about The Merriman Chronicles is available online

Follow the Author on Amazon

Get notified when a new books and audiobooks are released.

Desktop, Mobile & Tablet:
Search for the author, click the author's name on any of the book pages to jump to the Amazon author page, click the follow button at the bottom.

Kindle eReader and Kindle Apps:
The follow button is normally after the last page of the book.

Don't forget to leave a review or rating too!

For more background information, book details and announcements of upcoming novels, check the website at:

www.merriman-chronicles.com

You can also follow us on social media:-

https://twitter.com/Merriman1792

https://www.facebook.com/MerrimanChronicles

Printed in Dunstable, United Kingdom